POSSESSOR

DOMS OF MOUNTAIN BEND

BOOK 5

BJ Wane

Editors:
Kate Richards & Nanette Sipes

Cover Design & Formatting:
Joe Dugdale (sylv.net)

PUBLISHED BY BLUE DAHLIA

DISCLAIMER

This contemporary romantic suspense contains adult themes such as power exchange and sexual scenes. Please do not read if these offend you.

CONTENTS

Chapter One

Eighteen-year-old Randy Daniels sped down the dirt road in his pickup, the oversized tires spewing a cloud of dust that blew away in the wind. Tapping his hand on the steering wheel to the tune blaring from the radio, he thought life couldn't get any better than this moment. With his high school graduation behind him and acceptance into the University of Minnesota's agricultural degree program, he was riding high on exuberance for the future.

There were a few friends he'd grown up with he would miss when he left, almost as much as he would the family ranch and his horse. But he would return often. Minnesota wasn't all that far from Idaho, and nothing could keep him from home for long. His parents believed in a well-rounded education for their only child, and that included traveling someplace new once a year. After visiting over fifteen states, Canada, and a good portion of Europe, home on the ranch was still where he preferred to live after college.

Three months of summer, his favorite season, would come first. Randy planned to party hard with his girl, Patti, and his friends when not putting in hours at the feed store in Mountain Bend and keeping up with his obligations on the ranch. Their foreman, Steven, showed Randy no favoritism, and his father had instilled in him the value of hard work and importance of learning self-discipline. Of course, he thought with a rueful chuckle, that didn't mean he hadn't gotten into his fair share of trouble over the years, or hadn't earned more than a trip or two out to the woodshed.

Recalling his date last night, and the way he and Patti had steamed up the truck windows while parked on this same road, he shifted on the seat to ease his semi-erection. A few years ago, screwing around with a girl would have gotten him an earful from his dad and a worried look from his mother. Now, when or if they found out, the only thing either would say was to be careful and do the right thing, whatever that entailed. He wasn't serious about Patti, nor she about him. Nope, the woman he married would have to be someone special and have a lot of stamina in bed.

With Randy's big head and little head conversing and distracting him, he wasn't prepared for the bedraggled young girl who ran out into the road in front of him, waving thin arms to get him to stop. Slamming on the brakes, he swore and brought the truck to a halt just feet from her scrawny body. Before he could get his door open, she was there, yanking on the handle, her face red and sweaty, her breathing heavy.

Opening the door, she latched onto his arm with both small hands and tugged. "You have to come quick and help!"

"Whoa, kid. Why are you out here alone at your age?" he asked, sliding out from behind the wheel. Nudging his hat up, he scanned the acres of open fields on either side of the dirt lane, already knowing there were no houses or farms nearby. Looking down at the kid, he cocked his head, curious about her welfare. "What are you, seven, eight?"

Snapping gray eyes flashed up at him, followed by a belligerent tone. "I'm ten!"

His lips quirked. Damn, she was cute, all attitude and desperation. Still, he worried she was out here alone, far from a house or town.

"Sorry, ten. That's too young to be wandering around by yourself. Show me what you need help with then I'll give you a ride back to your parents."

A grimace tightened her mouth, but all she said was, "Come on. She's over here."

With speed and agility only a kid that young and gangly could accomplish, she sprinted across the road and over the wooden fence, her braided strawberry-blonde hair flying out behind her.

"Come on!" she called back with impatience.

Shaking his head, he caught up with her, regretting drinking so much at the field party last night. As pretty as the summer-green pasture with its smattering of colorful wildflowers was, the downed, skinny mare the girl led him toward cast a blight on the sun-drenched landscape and afternoon. He didn't see the spindly foal until they were a few feet from the pair and noticed the horse had already passed away, likely from a poor diet and lack of care, from the looks of her depleted body. The small colt hadn't fared much better than his mother before or after birth, from what he could tell of his too-thin frame.

The little girl dropped to her knees and ran a hand down his quivering neck then glanced around at Randy. "Can you help him?"

A hint of youthful vulnerability shone briefly in her eyes before she blinked, and the impatient snap returned.

"I can try." Squatting next to her, he gave the newborn an up-close visual inspection, determining it would take a lot of TLC, not to mention time and expense, for the colt to survive. "I'll take him home and have our foreman and vet look at him. It'll be up to them. His mama died giving birth, from what I can gather. You wait here while I pull the truck closer."

She grabbed his arm again as he made to rise. Desperation and fear were in her voice when she demanded, "Promise you'll come back? You won't take off?"

What kind of life had she led so far to make her so skeptical of an offer of help? Her dirty shorts and T-shirt were typical of someone her age out running around on a summer afternoon. She was thin but didn't appear malnourished. His concern came from her presence out here alone, so far from any houses. He'd spent the night with a friend in town after the party, and he was still a mile or two from the ranch.

"What's your name, kid?"

"Why?"

Randy sighed at the mistrust reflected on her

scrunched-up face. "Because I want to know who I'm helping."

"Oh. I'm Mickie. You're gonna take care of him?" Hope blossomed across her face, lighting her eyes, and producing her first smile.

Somehow, Randy didn't think it would be wise to say her name was as cute as her. "Yeah, I'm going to try. I'm Randy. Be right back."

It took him only a few minutes to find an opening in the fence and drive across the range. Getting as close as he could, he got out and lowered the tailgate before bracing to lift the solid black colt. Even in his depleted condition, the little guy was close to fifty pounds, which was no more than a bag of feed or haybale for him. But he didn't want to stress the animal out any more than his tragic beginning already had.

"Spread those blankets out, Mickie," he instructed, turning toward the back end of the truck. The foal gazed at him and the girl with wariness but was too weak to do anything except remain quiet and docile.

Mickie crooned to the horse as Randy settled him on the makeshift bed. He wanted to warn her about getting attached since he might not make it but didn't have the heart.

"Okay, kid. Hop out and get in the front. I'll drop you off at home first."

"No, I want to go with you." Belligerence crept into her tone as she added with a glare, "I found him, so he's my horse."

"Really?" Slamming the tailgate shut, he tried taking her arm, but she jumped out of reach, her mouth set in a mulish pout. "Do you have a barn, money for special feed, and for veterinary care?" A mortified blush stole over her face, and he felt bad for pointing out her limited circumstances, reminding himself she was just ten. "Yes, he's yours, but I'm offering to care for him for you, so cooperate, will you?"

She scowled, crossing her skinny arms across her skinny chest. "I'll agree to let you drive me home after I see where you're taking him. Otherwise, I'll walk."

The little minx probably realized he wasn't about to drive off and leave her out here by herself. "You strike a hard bargain, kid, but I agree. Now, get in the cab." He pivoted and strode to the driver's side, not surprised to see her already climbing in. Shutting his door, he said, "Put on your seat belt."

"Why?"

Randy rolled his eyes. Dealing with a stubborn

kid while nursing a hangover was starting to irritate him. "Because it's safer. Do it, or I'll let you walk."

She must have noticed the steel he'd injected into his tone because she obeyed without another word. Once he got going, he cast her a quick glance and asked, "For someone who shows a reluctance to trust others, you didn't seem to hesitate to flag down a stranger on a barren stretch of road."

Mickie shrugged, keeping her face toward the window. "You gotta do what's necessary to get by."

That kind of grit backed with a hint of despondency touched something in Randy, causing a pang to grip his abdomen. "What's your last name?" Maybe he'd heard of her family, and that could give him answers she wouldn't.

"Why do you need to know?"

Fuck, I don't need this. Whether he did or not didn't matter; he was stuck with the situation. "Kid, you could try the patience of a saint. If we're going to nurture that little guy back to health together, it would be nice to get to know you."

Whipping her head around, he eyed the swift change in her attitude from surly and cautious to delighted, and he returned her beaming smile.

"You mean it? I can help, watch him grow up?"

"Sure, he is your horse."

She hesitated then offered, "We can share him, if you want."

"*Mmmm.*" He pretended to mull over the suggestion. "I don't know as I'm an only child and never was good at sharing. It might be best if we say he's all yours." God, he hoped the colt lived.

"I don't have any brothers or sisters either, so it would be good practice for us." Shifting her gaze out the window again, she appeared to be pondering something, then she looked at him again and said, "My last name is Taylor."

Randy nodded, as if her concession wasn't a big deal when he knew it was. "Thanks." The name didn't ring a bell, but he could ask his parents. Reaching above him to the remote clipped on the visor, he pressed the button to open the gates onto their property. "Here we are."

Mickie sat up straight, her eyes wide as they drove down the long lane leading to his house. The barns and stable were visible from the sprawling, one-story brick home but were still a long hike.

"*Fudge*, Randy, don't you get lost in that house?" she asked, swiveling her head as he kept driving.

He sent her a rueful grin. "No, not after growing up there. Is fudge your clean version of the cuss word?"

Her slim brows tucked into a frown. "That's not a nice word, and I hate hearing it."

"Okay." There was more to that, but he was sure she would tell him it was none of his business, so he let it go. Steven came out of the stable as Randy pulled to a stop. "That's our foreman. I learned everything I know about livestock from both him and my dad."

Hopping out of the truck, he thought she mumbled something like, "Lucky you," but couldn't be sure. As much as he wanted to, he doubted he could break through her prickly attitude to pry.

Steven sent him a curious glance when Mickie dashed to the back of the truck without waiting for Randy. "She flagged me down on Old Mill Road and led me to this little guy." He jerked a thumb toward the truck bed where they both joined the kid.

The foreman let out a low whistle at seeing the colt. "He doesn't look good. Where's the mother?"

"Dead," Mickie responded in a flat tone. "Nobody took care of her."

"Then I'd say it's a good thing you came along, hon." Steven squeezed her shoulder, the look of compassion on his face mirroring the pang of empathy Randy experienced. "Let's get him bedded down in a stall, and I'll check our formula supply. I hope you two are up for a few weeks of mothering."

Randy opened his mouth to say she was too young for the responsibility, but one look at her determined, hopeful expression and he didn't have the heart.

"I can do it. I promise."

Lifting the colt out of the truck, he asked her, "How far do you live from here?" Steven opened the stable door, watching them both with interest, and Randy could see the same questions he had reflected on the foreman's face.

Mickie followed them inside, appearing unfazed by the excrement odor, her wide pewter gaze remaining glued to the foal as she replied with her usual defensive attitude, "I can walk here."

"I'm starting to think you can do anything you set your mind to, kid, but that doesn't answer my question." He lowered the colt and, with Steven's help, tried to get him to stand. Showing as much grit as the girl, the young horse made it about twenty seconds before going down.

"Let's get something in him. Mickie, you look like you could use something, too," Steven suggested.

Randy eyed her pale face and chapped lips, cursing himself for not paying closer attention to her needs. The fact she was so far from any homestead was enough to tell him her parents needed to step up and pay more attention to their daughter.

"Can I have a drink of water?"

"You can have a whole bottle," Randy answered gruffly, for some reason wanting to hug her. He almost grinned imagining her reaction were he to try. She stroked the colt's neck, the wistful look stealing over her face prompting him to say, "You found him, so you should name him."

"No kidding?"

The incredulous delight in her smile warmed Randy. He leaned against the stall door and crossed his arms with a nod. "No kidding."

Her face scrunched up as she mulled over possibilities then brightened seeing Steven return carrying a box with two water bottles, a large candy bar, and a bottle feeder for the foal.

"How about Black Jack? Do you like that one?" Her eyes clung to his face, as if his answer mattered.

"I think it's perfect. Steven?"

Steven smiled at Mickie, handing her the water. "Agreed. It's perfect for the little guy."

Randy let her stay and feed Black Jack before Steven reminded him someone might be looking for her, and the effects of his late-night partying were dragging him down. She wasn't happy about it but didn't argue when he ushered her back out to his truck an hour later.

"Where to, kid?"

"You can drop me off where we were."

"Try again, and don't give me any lip," he returned testily. "I'm taking you home."

Mickie shot him a scathing glare, huffed, then sighed in resignation. "Fine. The Crestway Mobile Home Park."

Randy frowned. On horseback, he could cut across the back field, through the woods, and over Mill Creek to reach the trailer court in less than fifteen minutes. But it was twice that far having to drive around the shortcut, and way too far for her to have walked where she'd flagged him.

"Do your parents know you took off so far?" He should have thought to ask her that earlier.

She let out a derisive snort, gazing out the window as he hit the road. "Don't worry, they won't care."

Her disgruntled voice was typical of a ten-year-old, but it still bugged him that he'd come across her wandering around all alone in a field. Between his head pounding and with tiredness tugging at him, he didn't have the energy to pull more answers from her right now. She remained quiet and sullen until he parked in front of the mobile home she pointed out and grabbed the door handle.

When she swung her head around, he couldn't resist the plea in her silver eyes as she asked, "Can I come back soon?"

"Sure, but only if I come get you, and you let your parents know. Deal?"

"Yeah, okay." She hopped down, surprising him when she tossed out, "Thank you, Randy. You made my day!" before trudging inside.

He shook his head and drove back home, wondering what he'd gotten himself into.

Three months later

Mickie leaned on the fence rail, her heart swelling with love for the first time as she watched Black Jack frolic in the corral. Randy had kept his word and let her help take care of the colt, riding over on his big roan a few times a week all summer to bring her to the ranch. She spent hours with either Randy or Steven, learning all about horses while nurturing her colt into a healthy, robust foal. She giggled, remembering their surprise when she insisted on mucking out Black Jack's stall, her irritation when Randy dared to say she wasn't strong enough, and her glee when she proved him wrong. He needed to quit underestimating her. She could, and would succeed in anything she put her mind to, which was a must if she ever wanted to get away from the trailer park.

She grimaced recalling the first time Randy had returned to take her to the ranch and refused to leave without meeting her parents. His brown eyes had turned hard when he'd been faced with their indifference, but, in all these weeks, he'd never said a word against them, or questioned whether she'd told them where she was going whenever he picked her up after that. Which was fine with her. The less she talked about her constantly arguing parents and was around to hear them going at each other, the happier she was. She supposed they loved her, in their cold, selfish way, but they sure as heck never showed it, or even expressed concern about her.

But that's okay, she thought, holding out an apple for Black Jack as he trotted over. She had another reason to do good in school and find a way to make it on her own when she was Randy's age. Her heart twisted every time he mentioned leaving for college. Even though he annoyed her when he turned bossy, and always wanted to know where she was, and what she'd been up to, Mickie would miss him, the rides on his horse, seeing his dark eyes light up when she showed him she wasn't the weak, scrawny kid he kept calling her.

More than that, she would miss hanging around the ranch so much after school started. Steven and both Mr. and Mrs. Daniels already offered to come get her on the weekends, and she hadn't hesitated to accept. The three of them were the adults she wished she went home to, and she tried hard not to envy Randy his good fortune or wish for what could never happen.

Wishing never got Mickie anything or anywhere. It was up to her to make her dreams come true.

Randy joined her at the corral, leaning his big arms on the fence next to her much thinner ones. "What are you looking so serious about, kid?"

Looking up at him, she experienced that funny catch in her throat she sometimes got when he was near. She lumped it in with all the other things about him that irritated her but she kept quiet about so he would still want her around.

"School. I wish it could stay summer."

He tugged on her braid, one of his habits she liked. "Between my mom, dad, and Steven, you can still spend weekend afternoons here. You can't stay gone for long. Black Jack would miss you." He reached out and stroked the colt's nose. "I gotta tell you, I didn't put his chances of survival very high. You did good, Mickie."

Her heart swelled with pride. Another thing she liked about him was his praises. No one had ever complimented her before, except teachers on her work. But they said the same thing to all the kids. Randy's words were just for her.

"Thanks," she mumbled, unused to feeling self-conscious or grateful.

"I gotta run. If I'm not back in time to take you home, Steven will drive you."

"Where are you off to?" And why did she care?

He winked at her. "I've got a date with Patti."

Mickie rolled her eyes. "You're going to break her heart when you leave for college. Why do you bother? You're leaving." She didn't understand why he wanted to go out all the time when he could be here, having so much fun on his ranch.

"You wouldn't understand. In a few years, you'll know why I bother."

"I doubt it. From what I've seen, no good comes of it. You'll see when a girl breaks your heart and you're unhappy, like my mom." Her mother often threw nasty remarks at her dad, blaming him for

DOMS OF MOUNTAIN BEND: Possessor

everything.

"One, no girl will break my heart because I don't get serious them. Two, don't compare everyone to your folks. You've seen how happy my parents are. A lot of couples have good relationships." Compassion shone in his eyes, a look she didn't care for. She didn't want to be pitied. "I'm sorry yours don't. They haven't been fair to you."

Mickie shrugged. No sense crying over what couldn't be changed. "I get by."

Four years later

Bending low over Black Jack's sleek neck, Mickie laughed as they raced across the pasture, the warm wind whipping against her face as the ground below whizzed by under the stallion's pounding hooves. She loved the way his muscles bunched against her legs, his heavy breathing matching hers. The first thing she'd done on the last day of school for the fourth year in a row was stay on the bus until it stopped up the road from the Daniels' ranch to let out the neighbor's kids. Steven always greeted her with a smile, and in the last two years, ever since Black Jack was old enough to ride, the foreman had him saddled and ready for her.

Life just didn't get any better than this, she mused, reining him in as they neared the stable. She loved listening to the cattle lowing in the pasture, the sight of the bright red barns and stables trimmed in white, Mrs. Daniels' lemonade and cookies, and Mr. Daniels' gruff but friendly "How ya doin', kid?" They welcomed her inside their big house that always smelled of home cooking and was filled with bright sunlight. Mrs. Daniels had insisted she come in out of the rain one day, and she spent the cloudy, gloomy afternoon letting Mickie help put together a meatloaf and potato casserole. Since then, her cooking skills had improved, along with her knowledge of ranching.

The Daniels ranch wasn't large, not compared to some Idaho spreads, but Mickie loved riding their two-thousand-acre rangeland, traversing the wooded areas, and letting Black Jack splash through the creek and pond. Randy and Steven would greet her return with lectures on going too far and staying gone too long, which she ignored. She even enjoyed mucking out stalls, keeping the tack oiled, and the aisle swept, but her favorite chore was grooming the horses.

The thing that endeared the Daniels and Steven to her the most, though, was when they started paying her last year, on her thirteenth birthday, after surprising her with a birthday cake and new saddle for Black Jack. Annoying tears pricked her eyes as she rode up to the stable yard, thinking about that day, and her good fortune. She had no use for tears, not even happy ones. The money she earned here she kept hoarded and secret from her parents, planning on using it for more education after high school.

She dismounted, patting Black Jack's soft, ebony neck, wishing she could just jump ahead through the next four years. Life would be perfect once she was grown up. But for now, she mused with a smile, hearing a truck rumbling up the drive, life wasn't too bad.

Randy was finally home from college for good instead of a few days or weeks during breaks.

Mickie swung the saddle off the stallion, listening as the truck door slammed shut, the funny tickle in her stomach when she heard Randy's deep voice unexpected. She was used to happy giddiness assailing her at seeing him again, but that sensation was new, and weird.

"There you are. Think you can take a minute away from that guy to greet me?"

She turned, her heart skipping a beat seeing him towering over her, his chocolate eyes twinkling, his mahogany-brown hair curling around his tanned neck, his scruffy whiskers giving him a rakish look. He was the same yet different, and she didn't understand why or how.

"Only a minute," she teased. "Some of us have work to do."

"Smart ass." He reached out and tugged her braid, and that funny sensation in her tummy returned. "Admit it, kid, you missed me."

"Maybe, depends on if you get bossy and nosy all the time again." She stroked her fingers through Black Jack's mane when he nudged her for attention, mostly to keep from touching Randy.

"Someone has to look out for you. Why don't you finish with Black Jack and come up to the house? All of the hands are joining us on the patio for a barbeque."

That was the first time he'd lumped her in with the five ranch hands in their employ, the pang of hurt feelings it gave her unexpected and unwelcome. "Sure," she said, turning around. "I'll be done shortly."

His large, heavy hand landed on her shoulder. "Everything okay, Mickie?"

"Just fine, Randy. I'm glad you're home."

Mickie *was* glad, maybe too happy. She sensed

things were about to change between them, and she didn't like that.

Chapter Two

Four Years Later

"The girl rides like the wind."

Randy didn't take his eyes off Mickie when he answered his dad. "Yeah, she does. Black Jack will miss her."

His dad smiled. "I will, too, as well as you."

"Well, *duh*, Dad." Shifting the straw blade in his mouth from the left to the right, Randy cast a quick glance at him, relieved to see him looking so good after suffering a mild heart attack less than a month ago. Not much could keep his dad down for long. "She's been a fixture around here for eight years. It's going to seem strange with her so far away for so long."

Mickie had been thrilled when she was accepted into a veterinary assistant program in Colorado. He could only imagine her parents' shock when she announced she was leaving. He was damn proud of the kid, the way she saved the money they had paid her these past few years and strove to keep her grades up, both a means to this end she'd craved ever since she started hanging around the ranch.

Watching her now, riding that stallion bareback, laughing as they galloped into the stable yard, he shook his head in bemusement. Her grit and determination never failed to amaze him, and he didn't know why. He should be used to how she wouldn't let anything get in the way of her goals. Hadn't she proved that the first winter after they met and an overnight snowstorm had kept him from picking her up the next day? He'd read her the riot act when one of the hands spotted her hitchhiking her way over here wearing a threadbare coat, her worn sneakers soaked through from trudging through snow.

It wasn't the first time he'd butted heads with her stubbornness and prickly attitude toward anyone who attempted to tell her what to do, but given her home life, he couldn't blame her. She wasn't used to anyone caring about her and didn't know how to handle it when he, or anyone else on the ranch tried to protect her from herself and from potential harm.

"You're going to have to drag her up to the house," Ron said, pushing away from the fence. "Your mother is ready to celebrate by feeding everyone. She won't stop trying to put some meat on the girl's bones."

Eyeing Mickie's long, denim-covered legs and toned arms as she slid off the horse's back, Randy thought she looked a lot healthier at eighteen than ten. If she would eat more and slow down once in a while, she might even put on some curves. He frowned, picturing the horny college boys he wouldn't be around to warn her against. She wasn't a kid anymore but still young and naïve when it came to guys.

"She might be better off staying skinny until she's done with school. You know how guys are at that age," Randy replied.

His dad chuckled and slapped him on the back. "I remember how you were back then, before and during college. Maybe it's a good thing she's leaving, so you won't be tempted."

Randy sent him an incredulous look, unable to believe his dad would even hint he would go there with Mickie. "She's too young for me, Dad."

"Look again, Son, but not too hard. Remember, it's her turn to head off to college. Go get her. This party's for her, and we can't start without her."

Shaking his head, watching his dad stroll away, Randy wondered what had gotten into the old man. He would always look at Mickie as the cute, neglected kid he and everyone else around here had taken under their wing, and regard her as family. He could no more consider any other relationship with her than he could fly to the moon. His astonishment changed to humor as he imagined Mickie's attitude toward the BDSM lifestyle he'd been exploring the past few years. No, he couldn't even go there long enough to picture her scathing expression at such an idea.

He'd never imagined the satisfaction he could get from seeing to a woman's needs, whether they were emotional, sexual, or a combination of both. It wasn't about sex, or rarely, yet he reaped as much pleasure from a scene without intercourse as he did when he took it that far. Now, he only went out on an occasional date with someone not in the lifestyle, and more often than not, ended the evening at their door.

With summer winding down, there was no end to chores and preparations for fall, but they always made time for special occasions. Mickie's eighteenth birthday and acceptance into college were two big ones, and Randy refused to let her get away with balking at socializing when they were getting together for her. It was bad enough she'd shunned his dad's big sixtieth bash last month, joining the party of about thirty people only long enough to give Ron a hug and grab a piece of cake.

He rounded the barn in time to hear her mutter, *"Fudge!"* and grinned at her continued bastardization of the curse word.

"Tsk, tsk," he teased. "Such language."

"Oh, bite me," Mickie replied with a wide smile, never pausing in running the brush down the stallion's neck. "Don't you have work to do?"

"Nope, and neither do you for the next hour. Come on, Mom's waiting for you." He knew what to say, never hesitating to use her fondness for his parents, especially his mother, as bait.

Mickie sighed, rolling her eyes. "You people and your celebrations. Hold on, I'm almost done."

Walking forward, Randy patted Black Jack's flank, admiring the healthy, beautiful stallion Mickie had a hand in rearing. "You've done good by him, kid. You'd never know this was the same foal you rescued from certain death."

Her gray eyes held a wicked gleam as she gazed at him over the horse's back. "You weren't so sure back then, of him or me."

"Newsflash, Mickie. I'm still not sure of you, like why you're putting off attending your own party. It's just us and the ranch hands today." Their smaller herd required fewer cowboys to attend it, and they only employed five extra hands besides him, Steven, and his dad, adding up to ten when they did roundups for auction.

"Fine." She huffed and turned to open the corral gate. After closing it behind the stallion, she shrugged. "Okay, let's get this over with."

Randy couldn't resist tugging her braid, the flush stealing over her cheeks a new reaction to something he'd done countless times over the years. Ignoring it and the way she averted her face, he admonished, "You can pretend to enjoy yourself. Mom made your favorite chocolate cake."

That got a spark of pleasure out of her. "Dark chocolate with fudge icing?"

"Of course."

Her face softened. "That was nice of her, and I always enjoy myself around your family. You know how limited my time is, and how I hate to spend it on frivolous stuff."

They strolled across the green lawn between the ranch buildings and the house, past the older small truck they'd given her two years ago when she'd gotten her license. "I don't consider eighteenth birthdays and heading off to college frivolous. I'm proud of you, Mickie. I'll miss you, though. We all will."

"Then you'll know how I felt when you took off."

He laughed, drawing heads toward them as they went around to the back patio. "You were happy to have me gone for a while because you thought you could go back to having no one to answer to."

"True, but I still missed you." She paused where they were, remaining out of earshot of the others. Placing her hand on his arm, she looked up at him with an expression he couldn't read. "You'll wait for me, won't you, Randy?"

Wondering at her earnest expression, he sought to soothe whatever uncertainties were going through her head. She'd never been away from Mountain Bend. "Sure. You should know by now I'll always be here for you. Come on, I'm hungry."

Mickie's heart went haywire as she stood in the shade of one of the towering pines the Daniels' had built their house around without removing any, unsure whether the sudden heat enveloping her was due to the warm afternoon temperature or Randy. The change in her body's reaction to his nearness or light touch had started about a year ago, and she still struggled with what to make of it. But even standing there in indecision, she couldn't help the elation sweeping through her at his promise. Knowing he would wait for her to return to pick up and forge ahead on a new path with their relationship filled her with indescribable joy.

Until she started looking at him as a man instead of the big brother she never wanted or the person who had befriended her and given her a whole new lease on life, she'd never been interested in boys or men. While she'd harbored fantasies of her and Randy doing things she couldn't fathom with anyone else these past months, she refused to let those newfound cravings derail her from her goal of an education that would get her away from the trailer park for good. She would never rely on anyone, not even Randy, to obtain and keep hold of that dream for her.

Randy's mother, Caroline, waved her over to the picnic table strewn with food, the grill behind her billowing smoke as Ron lifted the cover. The homey scene brought a lump to Mickie's throat as she started forward. The Daniels had welcomed her into their home eight years ago and every day since, giving her a safe haven to run to when she couldn't stand listening to her mother's bitter tirades against her father, blaming him for everything that was wrong with their lives. Watching him drown his own bitterness in alcohol more and more didn't help the tense situation.

Her parents hadn't acknowledged her birthday in years, but that was okay, she thought, eyeing the abundance of food then catching Randy's wink. She had all she needed here, and her dream of getting out of the trailer park was in the works.

"Mrs. Daniels, I told you not to go to so much trouble." Mickie braced for her hug then relaxed as she inhaled her familiar perfume mixed with the sweet scent of chocolate.

"Nonsense, Mickie," Caroline replied, releasing her. "You've been such a joy and bright pick-me-up around here, not to mention I needed a girl to cater to after dealing with these guys for so long."

Randy sent them both a derisive look over his shoulder as he took over at the grill. "She wasn't always a joy. More like a pain in the butt every time she took off and I had to leave off my chores to find her."

Mickie rolled her eyes. "And I told you on day

one I could take care of myself."

Cord, one of the hired cowboys, chuckled. "She's got you there, Randy. We've never had to rescue her from any harm."

Randy frowned. "You guys always stuck up for her, which only encouraged her to take risks."

"Nah," Mickie drawled, smiling at Cord. "I've never liked restraints put on me, is all."

A funny expression crossed Randy's face, one she couldn't decipher for a change, before it cleared as he handed a platter stacked with burgers to his dad.

"That's because you were raised without them," Ron said, his gruff tone underlined with affection. "Now, sit your scrawny butt down and eat, girl."

Mickie beamed at the older man. "Hey, I'm not scrawny anymore, not after all this time eating Mrs. Daniels' cooking."

She took a seat at the table, glad when Cord sat on one side of her, and Tim, his best friend, slid in on the other. Randy's nearness was proving too distracting in new and, she admitted, exciting ways, and she couldn't afford to let them sidetrack her from her goals. It was enough he promised to wait for her. His vow would see her through the lonely weeks ahead of missing him, the ranch, and everyone on it.

Steven slid a Coke across the table to her and raised his can in a toast. "To Mickie. Happy birthday, and best of luck in college, hon."

Fudge. Mickie blinked away the watery film in her eyes, wishing she could stay this week instead of returning home. But, she had packing to do, and even though her parents were neglectful, she tried not to follow in their footsteps. In the past few years, using some of the cooking skills Mrs. Daniels taught her, she strove to have a meal ready on the days her mother worked late cleaning offices in Boise, or when she pulled one of her disappearing acts for a few days, returning with no explanation. During those times, her dad worried her most, coming home drunk after leaving work at the mill and hitting the bars.

"Thanks, everyone."

Count your blessings, she told herself while gorging on the thick cheeseburger, potato salad, and chocolate cake. She refused to worry about her parents now, or when she left, or let how much she would miss *this* part of her life drag her down.

That was easier said than done when Randy walked with her to her truck a few hours later and she couldn't swallow past the sudden lump in her throat. His bulging biceps brushed her shoulder as he reached for the door handle, and another warm rush washed through her. She gazed at his familiar rugged face, his shadowed jaw, his sculpted lips that drew her curiosity about his kiss for the first time. So much so, she caught herself leaning forward, tempted to rise on her toes to reach him, before stepping away from that temptation. Not yet. She couldn't chance anything interfering with giving school her full concentration.

"Are you sure you don't want to stay for a few more weeks? Classes won't start for two months," he said.

"I'm sure. The roommates the college hooked me up with will be there about the same time, and since we found it cheaper to rent a duplex than stay in the dorm, there's a lot to do. Plus, I want to find a job as soon as possible."

Admiration and a touch of exasperation colored his voice as he replied, "You never let anything slow you down. Be careful you don't get burned out, Mickie. It can happen."

"No way." Unable to resist, Mickie threw her arms around his waist and hugged him. "I'll text you when I get there."

"See that you do," he returned in a deep, gruff rumble that vibrated under her ear.

Releasing him, she got into the truck and lifted her hand as he shut the door. Never in her wildest dreams had she imagined it would be so hard to drive away from Randy and the ranch her first chance at getting away from her home life. As she parked in front of their trailer and got out, she could already hear her parents arguing and resigned herself to another long night.

Four years later

"You just got home and you're leaving again," Mickie's dad, Ed, complained.

Mickie paused with her hand on the front door to glance back at him. Maybe if he'd get out of his recliner and do a few things around the rundown place, her mother wouldn't spend so much time away. Past experience told her he wouldn't listen to that advice or criticism, so she didn't waste her breath. Besides, she was chomping at the bit to get out to the ranch. She'd been too busy to return home much this past year. Okay, maybe that wasn't true. Too reluctant was closer to the truth. As much as she missed Randy, Black Jack, and everyone else, at school she didn't have to deal with this, with them. She'd called regularly, and couldn't help worrying, but couldn't say she'd missed either of them.

"Dinner's ready, Dad. All you have to do is heat it up. Mom gets off work soon."

"That don't mean shit. She's cheatin' on me again. I just know it."

If she was, Mickie wouldn't be surprised. Like he said, it wouldn't be the first time. "That's between you two. I'll be back later."

She left before he could say anything else, or her guilt for leaving him alone prodded at her to stay around longer. With her degree in hand, she had several decisions waiting to finalize, but they all hinged on Randy. College had been a blast, all of it due to the freedom of being away from home and her parents for the first time, and knowing Randy was waiting for her on the ranch. Even though she couldn't bring herself to return very often, too reluctant to give up the peacefulness of living without being in the middle of her parents' constant battles for even short visits, she'd spoken with Randy more in the last four years than the previous eight.

Mickie was riding high on her prospects for a bright future as she drove out to the ranch that had been more of a home for her than her own. As much as she'd missed everyone and Black Jack, though, she wouldn't have traded the last four years away for anything. She loved school, extending her curriculum to include animal husbandry, liked all her new friends, and had dated a few boys she'd grown fond of but who couldn't compare to Randy.

She smiled, remembering the times she had come home and listened to Caroline's disgruntlement with Randy's single status at thirty. Mickie was young but not stupid. She couldn't expect a man Randy's age to stay celibate while waiting for her, and she wouldn't know for sure if he was the one for her without dating. She couldn't bring herself to sleep with any of her dates, couldn't take things past some heavy petting before she would find herself craving Randy. Given the eight-year gap in their ages, she didn't begrudge him sowing his wild oats but now was ready to take him up on his promise to wait for her for a meaningful relationship.

They never spoke of that, either over phone conversations or during her short visits. Other than Randy lecturing her on being careful who she went out with and her teasing him by asking if he was careful , nothing was said about their dating others. She supposed it was just one of those unwritten rules she knew little about.

As Mickie went through the gates and saw the familiar ranch buildings and house, her pulse leaped with a wave of excitement. Maybe it was some perverse part of her psyche that had kept her from telling anyone other than her parents she was packing up to come home this weekend. One of her professors who also happened to be a traveling veterinarian had offered her her dream job, but she'd put him on hold until she spoke with Randy. The decisions awaiting her were overwhelming, and she didn't want to make any mistakes, or give anyone a heads-up in case they tried to put in their two cents.

She wanted everything on her terms or not at all. She'd spent too many years living, and suffering, from her parents flawed relationship and had enjoyed the independence and freedoms of being away and on her own too much to allow anyone a chance to sway her mind.

Mickie recognized the vehicles of the hired hands, but didn't see Randy's oversized truck. Her disappointment fled as soon as Steven emerged from the stables and a wide grin creased his weathered face. Other than his hair going gray, he hadn't changed much over the years. He was there when she opened her door and swept her up in a bear hug, his deep chuckle and twinkle in his blue eyes warming her insides.

"This is a hell of a surprise." Releasing her,

Steven put his hands on her shoulders and gave her a mock frown. "Why didn't you tell us you were back?"

"I wanted to surprise you. After I returned from my graduation trip – thank you again, by the way – it didn't take me long to move out." The Daniels, Steven, and the hired hands had all pitched in and given her a one-week vacation in Florida after hearing her roommate had invited her to join a small group headed to Pensacola.

"As happy as I am to see you, your timing sucks. The Daniels went to Boise, and the guys are riding the north pasture. Randy and his girl are with them."

Her heart sank, and an irrational spurt of irritation tightened Mickie's muscles. She'd been hoping to start their relationship, not wait on him to dump whoever he was seeing.

"I'm surprised he found one who can sit a horse," she returned with sarcasm.

Steven chuckled. "She couldn't until he taught her. He seems quite taken with her, though. They've been exclusive for a while. Caroline isn't thrilled with her, but is glad for him. Come on, you may as well say hi to Black Jack and take him out to join them. They'll all be happy to see you."

Obviously not Randy so much, she thought,

not caring for the pang in her chest. So far, this day was not going as she'd planned.

Black Jack whinnied as soon as Mickie entered the stable, the sight and sound of the stallion never failing to bring a lump to her throat. He'd grown into a magnificent equine, his coat a shiny ebony, his thick muscles and beautiful form a testament to his good health. No matter how many months passed without seeing her, he never forgot her.

"How's my big boy?" Mickie crooned, reaching up to stroke his head as he leaned over the stall gate and nudged her.

"Take him out, and I'll grab your saddle," Steven tossed out, walking toward the tack room in the back.

"Thanks," she returned.

The summer day was perfect for a ride, and Mickie wasted no time getting a bridle on Black Jack and leading him outside. Even though she wasn't happy Randy was with someone else, she still wanted to see him, let him know she was back. With luck, that's all it would take for him to ditch his current flame to start their future. Whatever Caroline or Steven had read into the relationship, she was sure Randy wasn't serious about the woman. In all these years, she'd never known him to get serious about anyone except her. Granted, his attitude toward her had always been that of an older brother looking out for a younger sister, but she'd been eighteen when he'd promised to wait for her, not the pathetic little kid he'd first befriended.

"Here you go, kid." Steven swung the saddle on Black Jack, who tossed his head and pawed the ground, eager for a run.

"When are you going to quit calling me kid?" Mickie frowned, hoisting herself up into the saddle then looking down at Steven. "I'm twenty-two years old."

"Since I'm old enough to be your father, you'll always be a kid to me, so deal with it. Have fun. See you when you get back." He stepped back with a smile.

As long as Randy didn't look at her that way, that was fine with her, she thought, nudging the stallion into a gallop as soon as they were past the fencing. Leaning over his neck, she whispered near his ear, "You and me, Black Jack, just like always." Racing across the wide open range with the wind hitting her face and the ground whirring by under his pounding, ground-eating hooves, she soon forgot about her annoyance and basked in the pleasure of being home again.

Mickie thought she should feel guilty for not thinking of her parents' place as home, but that she didn't was on them. She loved them, would do anything to help them, but was under no delusions about their single-minded focus on their dissatisfaction with each other. There were times growing up when she wondered if they even remembered they had a daughter.

It doesn't matter. With her future looking so bright, Mickie could forgive them for their neglect.

She veered into the woods and followed a favorite trail that came out at a creek. After letting Black Jack splash and get a drink, she returned to the range, enjoying the sun's heat on her shoulders as she rode north. Astride Cheyenne, his big roan, Randy sat taller than the other cowhands and was easy to spot when she reached the herd they were culling, selecting the cattle with the weight that would bring the highest dollar at the meat market.

Pulling Black Jack to a halt, her lip curled as she eyed the bleached blonde sitting on a blanket in the shade, her pale face reflecting boredom. If that was Randy's girl, Mickie doubted he was serious. He was an outdoorsman, through and through, the same as her.

A shrill whistle rent the air, and she swiveled to

see Randy heading toward her. Her pulse jumped, a reaction she only experienced when she saw him, and one that hadn't started until four years ago. Something had changed back then – hormones, maturity, or simply seeing him through the eyes of a woman instead of a young girl – whatever reason, it had stuck all this time, despite the long separations. The funny thing was, nothing else had changed between them, just that instant, flaming heat rushing through her body whenever he was near.

Clicking to Black Jack, she trotted to meet him halfway, ogling his tanned face, the dimples revealed by his smile, and the way his dark hair curled around his perspiration-slick neck and the coiled rope at his waist bounced against his thigh. He'd returned from college with the same bristled, unshaven look he still sported. Mickie didn't think it was possible for him to get bigger, but as he pulled alongside her, she swore his shoulders were wider, his forearms and biceps bulkier.

Remembering the other woman, she calmed her racing heartbeat and gave him a cool look. "Who is she?" she drawled, jerking her head toward the blonde.

"I'll introduce you. Damn, Mickie, it's good to see you." He reached over and yanked her braid, a gesture he'd done hundreds of times over the years, only this time the tug on her scalp sent prickles racing along her skin. "Why…"

"Because I wanted to surprise everyone," she interrupted him, liking the pleasure of hearing his voice and sitting there going damp with longing. "I was hoping we could hang out together." *Hint, hint.*

"Of course we can. I want to hear about your trip. We're about done here. Why don't you ride back with Melanie? I'll put something on the grill when I return."

Mickie struggled to keep her sarcasm and temper in check and failed. Was he clueless, or just trying to make the best of this awkward situation? "She can wait for you. Black Jack and I just got out, and we're not ready to return."

Randy thumbed his Stetson back and eyed her with a raised brow. "Is something wrong, Mickie? Everything okay with your trip back, and at home?'

She snorted. "Are things ever okay at home?" Blowing out a breath, she shook off her irritation. "Finish working, Randy. I'll see you in a bit."

Mickie turned Black Jack and kicked him into a run, lifting her hand to the cowhands as they sped by them. It bothered her how much she'd wanted to leap over and wrap herself around Randy, girlfriend or not. She had returned home ready to lose her virginity to him, but now had to rethink her plans, or at least put them on hold. And patience wasn't her strong suit.

****

Randy shook his head, watching Mickie tear across the pasture, fearless as ever, her red/gold braid flying out behind her. In all these years, he never had been able to figure the girl out, yet he remained quite fond of her. She was so young, full of life despite her rough childhood, and he still got a kick out of her prickly temperament, that attitude he wouldn't put up with from any other woman. He sent Melanie a wave, liking the way she was waiting for him, knowing she would be as biddable later at his place when he got her naked.

Joining the other hands, he separated a few more head for the auction as he imagined Mickie's reaction to his new, private BDSM club. He could no more picture her at such a place, minding the rules, than he could Melanie jumping in to help with the breech birth of a calf, like Mickie had done when she was just fifteen. Fuck, but he'd been proud of her that day, helping to save both cow and calf.

He'd missed her these past four years, her

return visits too infrequent and too short to spend as much time together as he wanted. He understood her reluctance to return once she was free of her stressful home life, and he remembered all too well how much fun college was. The fact she'd graduated at the top of her class proved she still possessed that single-minded focus on making something of herself, of forging her own future, an admirable trait.

"Hey, Boss," Cory said, riding up to Randy thirty minutes later. "It's good to see Mickie back. She owes me a rematch at billiards. Does that about do it for this group?" He jerked a thumb toward the separated cattle.

"Yep, we're good here. Let's drive them back down." Signaling to the other hands to head out, he asked Cory, "What's this about a rematch?"

"She beat the pants off me at the Christmas party and hasn't been back since. I can't let it stand at that."

Randy snorted. "Yeah, well, good luck. You know her competitive streak. I'll bring up the rear."

Steering Cheyenne toward Melanie, Randy wondered if she was a pool player then couldn't imagine his proper girl getting down and dirty with the guys, trading barbs and jokes while tipping a bottle of beer or bending over the billiards table to line up a shot. Melanie was Mickie's opposite in every way, quiet and reserved to her *in your face and if you don't like it tough* attitude, yet he was quite fond of them both.

"Are you done, then?" Melanie asked, getting to her feet as he reached out a hand.

He came close to chuckling, imagining Mickie's reaction were he to offer to assist her onto a horse. "For today. Ready?"

"Not to get on that thing again." She looked at the sweet mare he'd chosen for her to ride today with a look of disdain.

"You can ride up with me this time," he offered, reminding himself she was still green when it came to riding.

Her face paled as he lifted her in front of him, and he felt her shudder against his chest. "I'll take a car any day over this," she grumbled.

"Quit whining," he snapped, suddenly irritated with her.

"Or what?" Melanie gave him a coy look as he kicked the stallion into catching up with the others, confident the mare would follow.

"Or, instead of giving you the spanking you're wanting, you can go without tonight," he threatened, knowing he meant without the pleasure the light pain usually led to. She pouted and kept quiet until he dismounted in the stable yard and helped her down. The cowhands were already corralling the cattle slated for auction in the largest enclosure, the animals' lowing blending with the guys' shrill whistles and herding calls. All familiar ranch sounds on a summer day. He spotted Black Jack unsaddled and grazing in the field with several other horses but didn't see Mickie.

Leaning against him, Melanie traced one finger over his bicep, saying, "Tell me about the tomboy who stopped by on that big black horse. Who is she to you?"

"Jealous?" Randy didn't mention how ludicrous the very idea was.

She cocked her head. "Should I be?"

"No," he returned shortly. "We kind of adopted her around here ages ago. Mickie's a fucking fantastic rider and rancher for one so young, and I care a lot about her. She's special but not like you, baby."

Randy cupped Melanie's nape and drew her up for a deep, tongue-probing kiss, keeping her head immobile with one hand and her body still with a tight grip on one hip with his other. Innocent enough in appearances for public. He couldn't fathom why Mickie's disgruntled face popped into his head at the moment, but it was easy enough to shove the image aside and replace it with a picture of Melanie bound spread-eagle on his bed.

Well, now I know where I stand. Mickie inched away from the open stable door, opting to go out through the front after hearing that exchange between Randy and the woman he preferred over her. She scrubbed an angry hand across her watery eyes, refusing to shed a tear over him or anyone else. Crying over what couldn't be helped was a pathetic waste of time. Speaking of which, she thought, striding down the swept brick aisle between stalls, it was time for her to pull up her big girl panties and move on. This wasn't the first bitter disappointment in her life, and she would get over it as easily as she had others.

As much as she loved the ranch, Black Jack, and everyone here, she needed to forge her own path, find a place that was hers, not hang around someone else's home wishing it was hers for real. But why did that decision have to hurt so much?

Chapter Three

Seven years later

Exhilaration swept through Mickie as the difficult birth came to an end with the foal finally sliding from the mare's body. With gloved hands, she assisted the little filly's hind legs, its poor mother exhausted from the hours of labor and pain as Mickie worked to unwrap the umbilical cord from the foal's neck. There was nothing like the heady feeling of success, and she had Doc Adams to thank for her advanced veterinary skills.

Considered an expert in farm and ranch animals, Doc had offered her an internship her senior year in college and a job when she graduated. Between her education, the time she'd spent on the Daniels' ranch, and working for Doc, there wasn't much, if anything, she couldn't handle in running a spread, her ultimate goal.

"There you go, Mr. Dawson, another addition to your stables. From the looks of her, she'll be a beauty." Mickie gave the filly a quick onceover so as not to traumatize either of them and then stepped out of the stall.

"I appreciate you getting out here so fast, Mickie," Evan Dawson said as they walked out of the stable. "Especially this late at night. I worried I couldn't handle whatever was keeping Dancer from delivering."

"No, problem. I'm glad all went well." He held the truck door open for her, and she slid behind the wheel, tired and pumped at the same time.

"Drive careful, and I'll give Doc a call tomorrow."

She nodded with a smile. "Good night, then."

Starting the Honda Ridgeline, Mickie stifled a yawn as she got on the highway back to Littleton, where she'd lived for the last seven years. She spent a lot of time on the road driving out to ranches and farms to administer veterinary care, both when accompanying Doc and alone, when he couldn't get away from the clinic. It kept her busy, away from her apartment enough to keep her from getting homesick too often. Not that she hadn't returned to Idaho since moving away. She made it a point to visit her parents several times a year, and when she did, would arrange to see Caroline, Ron, and Steven. While she never planned to spend time with Randy, there was no way she'd let him, or any guy keep her from those she cared about or from her second home.

It was inevitable they would run into each other on occasion, but what irritated her most about those times was the longing that swept through her just seeing him again produced. Whether that need stemmed from missing his big brother friendship or the sexual itch that had popped up without warning back then she didn't know, and wouldn't care if it would disappear once and for all. But without fail, every time they encountered each other, her body turned warm, and her girly parts throbbed, leaving her with an indiscernible ache and in a bitchy mood. Like a cluster of small gnats invading her space, annoying her, she didn't like it, and certainly didn't want the tingling sensation association with him.

The long stretch of highway whizzing by while she drove cloaked under the star-studded inky Colorado sky lulled her into melancholy. To keep from nodding off, Mickie recalled the last time she'd seen Randy, and the first time she'd met his wife, Melanie, the woman she'd seen him with the day his words to Melanie had squashed Mickie's hopes of forming a new relationship with him.

Eighteen months ago

Mickie placed the last grocery sack in the back seat of her truck and closed the door. She always liked coming into Mountain Bend. The friendliness of the store owners where she shopped always brightened her day, and God knew she could use a pick-me-up today. She'd given her parents advance notice of her visit this week, but when she arrived late yesterday, her mother was supposedly still at work. Since she remained a no-show today, Mickie and her father were aware of the truth. Unlike her father, she didn't much care where or with whom her mother spent her nights other than the pain her infidelity caused her dad. What little attention she'd gotten as a child had come from him.

Discovering there were few groceries in the kitchen this morning, she'd headed into town earlier, already eager to get away from listening to her dad curse and complain about her mother. She took the time to stop by Cee Cee's salon for a visit with Chelsea, the only friend she'd kept in touch with from high school. After taking her up on an offer of a trim, she bought a maple-scented candle at Anna Lee's Candle and Gift Shop, hoping it would help dispel the trailer's musty odor, then went grocery shopping. Picking up the to-go order she'd phoned in earlier was next, and she hoped surprising her dad with his favorite dish, chicken fried steak, would improve his mood.

Driving the two blocks to Mountain Bend's steakhouse, the only dining establishment that wasn't fast food or bar offerings, she tried not to let her parents' volatile, inexplicable relationship get her down. That was easy enough when she was in Colorado, but difficult when she returned, even for short periods. Had she been paying more attention to her surroundings, instead of bemoaning her parents' dysfunctional relationship, she might have been better prepared for seeing Randy and his wife exiting the restaurant as she parked in front of the renovated old mining company.

"Well, fudge," she muttered, eyeing the blonde clinging to his arm and gazing at him with a look that hinted at a willingness to do his bidding.

It hadn't taken long for the rumors about Randy's private club to reach her ears a few years ago, or for her to research what he was into. Her lip curled as she imagined Melanie kneeling at Randy's feet, addressing him as Sir, keeping quiet and spreading her legs whenever he commanded. She'd dodged a bullet there, unable to comprehend why any woman would submit to a man's bidding, swearing she was glad Randy's sexual interest hadn't included her. She'd rather remain the kid he'd befriended than try to be something or someone she wasn't just to win his favor.

Which didn't explain the heat suffusing her as she got out of her vehicle and caught his attention. As soon as his dark-chocolate eyes landed on her, her pussy fluttered, and her nipples peaked. As much as she enjoyed sex, she'd never reacted with such a strong sexual tug toward any other man, not even those she'd slept with. Of all the hip-swaggering, loose-limbed striding, Stetson-wearing cowboys she'd clamped eyes on since reaching maturity, only Randy's tall, broad-shouldered, muscled body, and searing gaze could ignite instant arousal.

What the heck was up with that?

As he came toward her with a heart-stopping smile creasing his tanned, dark-bristled cheeks, Mickie almost caved to the temptation to leave. But she wouldn't let him, or any man keep her from her home, and she wouldn't allow her wayward libido to dictate her life.

"Mickie." Pleasure infused his voice. "Why

didn't you let me know you were back?" Randy disengaged Melanie's clinging arm and pulled Mickie against him for a bear hug.

No, no, no! His wife is standing right there, for God's sake! *She pulled away from his comforting hold and stepped back, berating her stupid, hormonal driven body.* "I just got in last night and won't be here long." *Turning to Melanie, she held out her hand.* "Hi. I'm Mickie."

One slim brow winged up as Melanie barely touched her hand. "Melanie Daniels. Is that a nickname?"

Mickie's lip curled at the derision etched on her face. As if she cared what Melanie, or anyone else thought. "If it is, I don't know for what. Whenever Mom or Dad decided they should talk to me, it wasn't about my name." *She eyed the other woman's curvy figure showcased in a bright- pink summer dress, her heels adding length to her already long legs. Yep, she mused, quite comfortable in her old jeans, boots, and T-shirt, she'd definitely dodged a bullet with Randy. Turning her head up to him, she caught the scowl he sent his wife and took pure feminine pleasure in it.* "I'll try to come by before I go. Good seeing you again."

"How about tomorrow afternoon? We'll go for

a ride," he suggested.

Mickie started to give him an excuse, but the angry glare Melanie sent him caused some perverse part of her to accept, just to rile her further. "Sure. I'll call when I'm on my way. Nice to meet you, Mrs. Daniels," she added in a sugary tone that made Randy's lips twitch.

She'd just entered the restaurant when fingers curled around her arm, long nails digging into her skin as Melanie jerked her around to face her glare. "Don't bother coming out to the ranch tomorrow. Randy has me now, and you're not needed around there anymore."

She'd never thought so highly of herself as to believe her visits to the Daniels' ranch were ever about being needed, but this woman didn't deserve to know that since Randy hadn't stopped his wife from this confrontation. Masking her anger and her hurt, she lifted Melanie's hand off her arm with a look of disdain.

"No problem. I certainly wouldn't want to go where I'm not wanted. You can run along to do your husband's bidding now." Mickie pivoted and strolled to the checkout counter for her order without looking back again.

Mickie had canceled their ride after that confrontation with Melanie when she informed her she wasn't welcome anywhere near her husband. Instead of getting into a cat fight right there in public or putting Randy in an untenable position, she'd walked away. She couldn't imagine anyone more ill-suited for Randy, but what did she know about his tastes other than they didn't run in her direction? Last she heard, Randy and Melanie divorced less than a year later, and he had taken off somewhere. Mickie hadn't seen him since, and they'd spoken only twice on the phone, her birthday and Christmas.

Pulling into her apartment complex, Mickie yawned, eager for bed. Thinking about that day and the last time she'd seen Randy had put her in a grumpy mood, which worsened when she awoke at the crack of dawn to her cell buzzing and saw her dad's name on the caller I.D.

"Dad, why are you up so early?" she asked, rolling over in her double bed, wishing she had a better view out the bedroom window other than the parking lot.

"She's gone." His voice broke on a tortured sob, which alarmed her more than his words.

Sitting up, she flung the covers aside. "Who? Mom?"

"Yes, of course. Her clothes, everything. You need to come home. I can't handle this alone," he insisted.

She sighed and rubbed her brow. "She'll come back; she always does."

"Not this time. She left a note, said she'd had enough and found something better, which means someone."

The bitterness and worry in her father's voice came through the phone, and Mickie didn't know whether she wanted to snap at him or try to soothe his wounded feelings. He was weak, lazy, and temperamental, but he was her parent. She never understood why she felt guilty for her parents' troubled relationship, but nothing about her family dynamics made sense.

"Dad, I can't just..."

"You have to, Mickie. You know I can't do as much since I went on disability."

She wondered how long it would take him to play his trump card. A fall at the mill last year had dislocated several vertebra in his lower back and left him unable to continue working on his feet all day and worsened his attitude and outlook on life, which he took out on everyone who tried to help. Since he'd hit the bar at lunchtime, his only compensation was a small stipend from workman's comp. Sensing the inevitable, she couldn't help but try one more time.

"I can't turn my back on Doc after all he's done for me."

"But you can your old man, is that it?"

Fudge. He knew just what to say to cause a cramp of guilt. What choice did she have? "I'll talk to Doc this morning and call you back."

****

"I'm going into town to get a few things. Do you need anything?"

Mickie picked her purse up off the sofa and turned toward her father. The cramped space of the trailer with its musty odor was getting to her, along with his belligerent attitude. He'd changed since her mother had left two weeks ago, and not for the better.

"Pick me up a few six-packs," he replied from his slumped position on the worn recliner.

Shaking her head, she tried to curb her frustration. "Forget it, Dad. I don't have the extra money, and you aren't eating well. The last thing you need is more alcohol."

"Don't sass me, girl," he snapped, glaring at her. "How could I eat with no one here to cook? Now that you're back, I can eat better. What are you fixin' for tonight?"

This was what she'd been afraid would happen when she returned – he would expect her to take her mother's place, demanding she wait on him hand and foot. Not going to happen.

"Meatloaf," she tossed over her shoulder, walking to the door. "But we need to talk. I'm not here to cater to you." She left, shutting the door on his angry tirade about the injustices of his life.

Sucking in a deep lungful of fresh, spring air, she lifted her face up to the sun's warmth, and took a moment to get herself under control. Doc's understanding and support had come close to unraveling the suppressed emotions of a lifetime of dealing with her parents, but she'd managed to keep herself in check. If she broke down over spilled milk, there would be no one other than her to clean up the mess, so why bother?

Unbidden, Randy's face flashed in her mind, a reminder of his and his family's friendship and support over the years. Yet, she mused, driving into Mountain Bend, here she was, still coping alone with whatever life threw at her. *It was your choice to run away with your tail between your legs*, her nagging, inner self pointed out. Too bad she couldn't tell that voice it was wrong.

"Suck it up and move on," she lectured aloud. Randy was off who knew where, still licking his wounds and mourning the end of his marriage to that twit. Oh, she could call him, or Steven, or the Daniels and enlist their help with finding a job and even with dealing with her father. But when she'd opted to stay in Colorado after college, she'd vowed not to lean on anyone again. She would either make it on her own or not. At least Doc had been generous enough to promise her a job if she decided not to stay. She was giving herself a month to get her dad more self-sufficient. If that miracle occurred, she could return to Colorado without guilt.

As she approached Mountain Bend's city limits, she slowed to watch a herd of gazelle run across the range, never tiring of seeing their graceful leaps, marveling at how fast they could run. Colorado's terrain and wildlife were so similar to her home state that living there didn't mean she had to give up what she liked best about Idaho's landscape. In fact, the only negative about Colorado was the hordes of people, even in the more rural towns.

Mountain Bend's shopping district consisted of one street, one over from its business district where century-old buildings had been restored and converted into the sheriff's department, city hall, and the prosecutor's office. Mickie spotted a new ice cream parlor next to the library as she turned off of Main, an incentive to shop fast and treat herself. Parking in the lot next to the city park, she started down one side of the street and worked her way up the other side, checking off her list and wincing as the cost kept adding up. Her mother never had been big on keeping up with the trailer, and, after taking an inventory of necessities, she'd discovered her mother had left her dad with very little.

By the time she stowed everything in her truck with the only thing left on her list to pick up her dad's prescription for his back pain, she was ready to check out the new ice cream parlor and delay returning home a little longer. She locked the door and turned, halting when she spotted Caroline coming out of the library. Just seeing her again brought a lump to her throat. She didn't miss her mother, didn't much care she was gone except for her dad's pain, but she'd really missed Caroline.

"Mickie!" Caroline came rushing across the street and enveloped her in a hug. "Why didn't you let me know you were visiting?" Her face clouded over with sadness. "Oh, dear, I'm sorry about your mom. Is that why you're here, to help your dad?"

"Yes, at least I'm trying. I'm sorry, I haven't had time to get in touch."

"I understand and wish I could be of some help. I took him a casserole last week."

That was just like her, always thinking of others. "Thanks, I'm sure he appreciated it. I was headed to get an ice cream. Can you join me?"

"Love to! How long are you staying?"

"I'm not sure, maybe a month. A lot depends on Dad, and finances. Dad's not good at managing his, and mine are limited since I had to quit my job to make this trip. I couldn't leave Doc hanging." If only she could harden her heart, life would be easier.

Caroline opened the door to the ice cream shop, giving her a smile Mickie didn't trust. "You know, dear, you could be the answer to our prayers."

Mickie smirked and followed her inside. "I've been a lot of things to different people, but never that."

"There's a first time for everything," she answered airily. "Let's get a cone and eat it in the park, and I'll explain."

Curious but still not trusting her, Mickie ordered a double scoop of rocky road then ribbed Caroline when she asked for the tutti-frutti. "What are you, twelve?"

"What can I say? It's my favorite."

They thanked the young girl behind the counter and stepped back outside, licking fast as the ice cream softened.

"Maybe we should have stayed in to eat them. They'd last longer," Caroline said as they settled at a picnic table under a tall spruce in the park.

"Where's the challenge in that?" Mickie bit into the top scoop and crunched on a nut. "Yum."

Caroline chuckled. "You always did like a challenge, starting with Black Jack. Drove Randy nuts."

"Lots of things about me drove your son nuts. So, how can I help you, Caroline?" Mickie was curious about her earlier remark.

"You know Steven has wanted to retire and is only waiting so Ron and I can go on our trip. So far, we haven't interviewed anyone we think can fill his shoes, especially since Ron has retired altogether from the physical requirements of running the ranch. You would be perfect for the job."

Stunned, Mickie could just stare at her across the wood table, her heart thudding out of control. Manage the ranch she loved, her home away from home, her safe haven during her teens? Her dream job just handed to her? There had to be a catch.

"What about Randy? Surely he'd come home if you told him Steven was ready to retire. I know how concerned he was about Ron when he had that heart scare."

Caroline shook her head, lowering her eyes, which added to Mickie's suspicions. "He's helping his cousin down in Texas, putting in a new irrigation system. Chase is my sister's youngest, and just getting his place going. He really needs Randy's help right now. Randy will come home when he's ready."

Watching her closely, Mickie bit into her cone then said, "Poor guy. His wife really did a number on him if he's still not over her."

"He doesn't talk about it, or her, but I suspect it's more his error in judgement in choosing Melanie in the first place that's bothering him now. Men and their egos." She wiped her lips with a napkin after swallowing the last of her cone. "What do you say, Mickie? Will you at least talk to Steven about it? We leave in two weeks and will be gone a month. If you're not happy when we return, we'll work something else out."

Mickie couldn't turn away from the hopeful look on Caroline's face or stifle her excitement at the offer. Even though she'd gotten over her infatuation with Randy years ago, the job would be easier, and more enjoyable without him around. If he did return, they wouldn't need her and there was always Doc's offer in Colorado.

"I'll come over in the morning, if that's good for you."

"Perfect!"

****

Randy rolled away from Shari's clinging body and groped for his phone on the nightstand as it rang. Seeing his parents' number on the lighted caller ID, he silently thanked them for the excuse to leave her bed.

"Gotta get this," he said, rising and walking out of the room with nothing but the phone. Padding down the hall into the kitchen, he answered in a voice scratchy from sleep. "Hey, good morning. I thought it was my turn to call you."

"It was," Caroline answered, "but we wanted you to know as soon as possible we've hired a new foreman who can start right away. Now you can stay and finish helping Chase since there's no need for you to come home while we're gone."

Using his free hand, he flipped on the coffeemaker and reached for a cup, curious about this turn of events. Last he'd heard from them, they didn't have any prospects to take Steven's place.

"Who is he? Have you checked his credentials and work history?" He wouldn't trust putting the ranch or his parents' well-being into the hands of a stranger.

"She, and yes, she has impeccable credentials and experience, the best. Steven's quite pleased."

The smugness in his mother's tone drew his suspicion. There was something she wasn't telling him. "Give me her name, and I'll do some digging, just to make sure."

"I'm sure you're not insinuating your father and I can't be responsible for hiring our workers."

Ouch. Randy winced at the cool rebuke. He might be thirty-eight years old but she could still put him in his place with a few words uttered in that frigid voice. "You know that's not what I meant."

"Well, I hope not. Anyway, all is well here, so no need to come home before we leave. We're confident the ranch will be in good hands, and Steven will only be thirty minutes away in Boise. Like he keeps telling us, he's retiring, not disappearing from our lives. Oh, and did I tell you? Betty talked old man Sanders into the two of them joining us!"

Randy almost choked on his sip of coffee hearing that. Sheep farmer Sanders had been a grumpy recluse since his wife's death a few years back, and he recalled his mother mentioning her best friend, Betty, and Sanders were getting friendly but never imagined them that chummy.

"Miss Betty must have the patience of a saint to take him on."

"You've met Poppy, his new manager. She gets the most credit. Poppy doesn't let anyone walk all over her, including her boss and her husband, Dakota Smith."

Randy chuckled. "She's a lot like Mickie. I met all three of their wives at the weddings."

He leaned against the counter and sipped his coffee again, unmindful of his nudity as he thought about Mickie who had become part of his family over the years, and his friends to whom he had sold his private club. There was a lot he'd missed since leaving almost a year ago, and it had been difficult making contact with any of them on his short visits home, but he'd managed to make their weddings. At least with Mickie, he'd tried harder. She was the one who called off their ride the last time they were both in town, a few months before the divorce. He remembered his disappointment had rivaled his irritation when she wouldn't give him a reason.

"Yes, she is. We hear your club is doing well

under the new owners," Caroline stated.

Randy winced, never comfortable talking about Spurs with his parents. "That must mean the gossip grapevine is thriving. I knew they were a good choice to sell to, and that's as far as I'm discussing the club with my parents."

Caroline laughed. "You were always the one uneasy with us knowing. Like we said, as long as it's legal and consensual, it's your business, just as our sex life is our business. Guess who I saw yesterday?"

"Mom, it could be literally anyone. Save some time and tell me."

She released a dramatic sigh. "You used to be more fun."

That was before I thought I knew what I wanted, got it then lost it. Funny thing was, in the past year since he'd discovered Melanie's betrayal, he'd come to realize he didn't miss her near as much as what he'd thought they had together – the perfect Dom/sub marriage, a relationship based on trust and a need the other could assuage.

"I'm still fun. Who did you run across?"

"Our girl, Mickie. She'll be around for a while, helping her dad since her mother has taken off for good, it seems."

Poor girl. The Taylors' neglect of their only

child had angered him over the years, but regardless of their parental indifference to her needs, Mickie had always tried to be there for them. An admirable trait that went unappreciated by both mother and father. It was no wonder she'd grown up with an attitude and had made a life for herself away from them.

Hell, Randy mused, he'd missed her more than his wife these past months, and the years before that. Her return gave him another reason to head home.

"I'll come home, just to make sure her old man doesn't get out of line, or run her into the ground, and to meet this new foreman."

"Not necessary, but you'll do what you want. I gotta run, sweetie. We'll call right before we leave. Love you!"

When she hung up, Randy realized she hadn't given him the name of the new foreman, but it would have to wait until he got to the ranch. Shari entered the kitchen wearing his T-shirt and eyeing him as if he were a piece of candy. Her recent possessiveness had made the decision to end things with her easy. He'd stayed celibate since divorcing his faithless wife a year ago, and made sure Shari was aware he was only in this for the physical gratification. Callous? Maybe, but at least he was honest.

He turned to rinse his coffee cup, saying over his shoulder, "I'll need my shirt. It looks like I'm headed back home sooner than I planned and will be leaving right away." And he didn't want to leave behind any part of him with her.

Shari pouted and pulled his shirt over her head as she came toward him. He recognized the gleam of lust in her eyes and braced himself to turn her away. He had at least a week's worth of work with his cousin before he could bail on him, and then packing and driving back to Idaho would take several more days. While he trusted his parents' good judgement in hiring, he refused to leave the ranch in a stranger's hands while they weren't around to oversee everything. It baffled him how either of them could have such blind faith in this person already.

"Let me please you one more time, Master Randy," Shari purred, going on her toes to brush her lips over his, placing one hand against his heart and wrapping the other around his cock.

"Sorry, baby, I don't have time. Be good and don't make a scene. I told you last night would be our final." Randy gripped both her wrists and removed her hands from his body, breathing a sigh of relief when she moved back without a fuss. Then she tossed his shirt in his face.

"Fine. Get out and don't come crawling back when you can't find someone else around here to do your bidding."

Chuckling, he pinched her chin. "Since I'm not staying around here, shouldn't be a problem. What?" he mocked, seeing the startlement cross her face. "Did you think I was making that part up?"

"It crossed my mind," she admitted with a scowl.

Randy stepped around her and put on his shirt, thinking how little she knew him after two months. "I'll get my clothes and let myself out."

Five minutes later, he walked out into the Texas heat, got in his truck, and drove to Chase's spread. For the first time in a year, he was returning home with enthusiasm instead of regret.

Chapter Four

" Damn, girl, you and that stallion still ride like you were kids."

Steven grinned from ear to ear, taking Black Jack's reins as Mickie dismounted with a quick laugh. *Fudge* but she felt exuberant with her blood pumping fast and her muscles quivering from exertion. Riding the herds, checking crop yields, and then racing back to the stable yard on a gorgeous summer day – did it get any better than that? She thought of her father's anger over her taking this job, his complaints all week even though she made sure his food was ready except for heating every morning before leaving and still returned to his surly disposition every evening. He was getting harder and harder to be around, let alone please and tolerate. If it weren't for this opportunity Caroline had given her, she'd return to Colorado, guilt or not.

Mickie patted the stallion's neck, his muscles

and stamina just as strong at twenty as at five. A horse's lifespan ran between twenty-five and thirty years, but she intended for Black Jack to be among the rare equines who stuck around much longer.

"That's because we're still kids at heart, aren't we, boy?" She kissed his soft nose and received a headbutt in return. "Ned and Toby are bringing in an injured calf – got caught up in some barbed wire off old fencing. Lance and Chad are collecting it and searching for any more before coming in."

Squeezing her shoulder, he replied, "They've taken a shine to you, which I knew they would. You're going to do fine without me around all the time."

Tears pricked her eyes, but like always, she blinked them away. The ranch wouldn't be the same without him, just like it wasn't without Randy. But she still loved it and her job.

Averting her face, she uncinched the saddle, saying, "Even so, I'll still harass you if you stay away too long. And the guys are what, eighteen, twenty? They take a shine to any female at that age."

The young cowboys working for the Daniels when Mickie had first met them had long since moved on, just like her before taking Caroline up on her offer.

Steven opened the corral gate for her and slapped Black Jack on the rump as he trotted inside to join two mares. Slinging an arm around her shoulders, he gave her a fatherly hug. "True, but they're doing good by you, and that counts. What are your plans this weekend? Please tell me you're going to get out and have fun."

Mickie hugged him back, hiding the blush creeping up her neck and covering her face in warmth. She didn't embarrass easily, but going to a private kink club wasn't something she wanted to discuss with someone who had been more of a parent to her than her own.

"I plan to catch up with some friends," she answered, pulling away from him with that partial truth.

Mickie assumed she would know at least one member of Spurs given the club was the only social venue between Mountain Bend and Boise. Not that she ran around with girls into the alternative sex practices, but it was either give the place a try to spend a few hours away from the trailer, or go into Boise where she was certain not to run into anyone she knew.

Then there was her curiosity about Randy's interest in a sexual lifestyle she just didn't get. When her desperation to escape her father's constant, bitter tirades and complaints this week had reached the breaking point, she'd gone over her Friday night options and looked up Spurs' website. While all the rules didn't appeal to her, she found herself drawn to the calm contentment that appeared etched on the women's faces in pictures, and the closeness they seemed to share with the men that wasn't entirely sexual. She didn't understand it but envied it enough to apply for a guest pass, answering honestly the question about her interest and writing it was purely social. Her surprise when that was accepted gave her the jitters and made her wonder what she'd gotten herself into.

"Good for you," Steven said then glanced across the field where Mickie noticed the hands coming in, Ned carrying the injured calf across his lap. "We better get a stall ready so you can treat him."

"I'll get my supplies." Mickie lifted a hand to the guys as they rode in and told Ned, "Follow Steve with him, will you? I'll meet you in the stall."

"Sure thing, ma'am," he answered with a teasing grin.

All of them knew she disliked that term as it made her sound so old. Naturally, they continued to use that address. "Keep it up, smartass." All the guys laughed, and she liked they didn't walk around on eggshells around her, and didn't resent answering to a woman. Her days here on the ranch this past week had been so much more pleasant than spending the days prior with just her dad for company. With luck, she would find enough to amuse and entertain her at Spurs tonight without getting involved with anyone or in the sexual escapades the private club catered to. Maybe she was being naïve about her expectations in checking out the place, but it was better than going back to the trailer and enduring her dad's surly company for several more hours before going to bed.

Mickie didn't wear shorts often, her job with Doc and on the ranch requiring long pants, but she stopped at the trailer long enough to change and eat something with her dad. She didn't want to stand out at the club, and even though she was given a pass for tonight on the strict dress code that required women to wear skin-revealing clothing, she'd thought meeting them halfway by wearing shorts would work in her favor. It was odd to think sitting around in shorts would keep her from getting noticed or propositioned by one of the men. Given some of the pictures she'd viewed and the fetish clothing she'd looked up, she guessed the men with dominant proclivities would be drawn toward those in skimpier, see-through attire, or who portrayed a more subservient attitude.

She went right into her room upon entering the trailer, lifting a hand to her dad who was sitting in front of the television, like usual. "I'll be right out, Dad, after I change."

"Hurry up, girl. It's going on seven, and I'm hungry," he grumbled.

Rolling her eyes at his laziness, she closed the bedroom door, took a quick shower, and changed into her white shorts and a gray-and-white striped tank before re-braiding her hair. After applying mascara, her one concession to makeup, she padded out to the miniscule kitchen, sighing when she spotted the dirty dishes in the sink.

Retrieving the chicken parmigiana from the refrigerator, she slid it into the oven before letting her irritation show as she snapped, "You could have at least rinsed these off." Picking up a plate and starting to scrub at the dried cheese stuck to it, she didn't hear him come up behind her until he spoke.

"Don't nag me about doing your job. I had enough of that from your mother."

She swung her head around and glared at his ruddy face, sick and tired of him feeding her that line. "And if you don't want me to walk out on you, too, I need you to start helping yourself. I can't, won't do it all, Dad."

"No one asked you to." He took a seat at the small table and returned her direct stare.

He was the only person Mickie refused to argue with, and that was because she'd recognized the futility of it long ago. "You've got ten minutes until that's hot."

They ate in silence until she finished, stood, and put her plate in the dishwasher, saying, "I'm going out. I don't know when I'll be back." She made to walk by him, but he startled her by grabbing her arm in a bruising grip.

"Where are you going?" he demanded.

Furious, she ground out, "Release me." When he didn't, she twisted her arm free, rubbed at the redness, and stormed from the trailer, ignoring him calling after her.

In all these years, he'd never touched her in anger or frustration. As she drove out to Spurs, Mickie calmed her racing heartbeat and managed to forgive him, deciding it was the stress of her mother leaving that made him worse to get along with than usual. Added to the back injury that forced him out of his position at the mill, he was dealing with a lot.

He needed time and her patience, but she would only give him so much of each and only put up with so much in the meantime.

The renovated, two-story log building nestled in a tree-surrounded copse off the main highway wasn't what Mickie had been expecting. In the outdoor lighting, it looked more like a rustic lodge, and she found the structure appealing and inviting, the number of vehicles in the gravel lot rather intimidating. She'd never imagined so many belonged to the exclusive establishment. Just how desperate was she for the diversion of a pleasant evening socializing and satisfying her curiosity about Randy's interest?

Opening the truck door, she eyed the lingering redness on her arm in the interior light, gritting her teeth against the soreness as she moved her fist in a circular motion at the wrist. Pretty damn desperate, she decided.

Mickie wasn't a shy person, and it took a lot, or a surprise, to make her uncomfortable. But as she entered Spurs large foyer and caught a glimpse of the interior club room through the open door leading into it, she paused as a wave of embarrassed insecurity hit her.

Reality is a heck of a lot different than computer

images and information, she mused, eyeing the bare breasted woman with her cuffed wrist attached by a short chain to her partner's belt loop with disbelieving disdain. She didn't begrudge or judge those whose idiosyncrasies she didn't understand or adhere to, but witnessing a woman's subservient disposition in this day and age baffled and confused her, stirring her anger as well as her curiosity as to what could possibly motivate them.

"You must be Mickie Taylor." A dark-haired woman came forward, her brown eyes warm with welcome as she held out her hand. "I've been watching for you. I'm Skye Trebek, here to show you inside and introduce you around."

Mickie returned her smile, her tension easing as she took her hand. "Thanks. I admit I'm way out of my depth as to the ins and outs of all that." She waved a hand toward the large playroom. "I'm just here to socialize, meet a few local people since Mountain Bend doesn't boast much of a chance to do either of those."

"So, you're new to the area?" Skye asked, leading the way inside.

"No, not at all. Born and raised here, but I've lived in Colorado for the last seven years, making only short trips home, and have lost touch with most everyone. Oh." She stopped in her tracks as she took in the odd equipment lining the sides of the room and the people bound on them, the sultry beat playing from hidden speakers adding to the eroticism. "How long does it take for someone to shed their inhibitions enough to let some guy do that?" She nodded toward a bench and the woman strapped facedown, her butt glowing bright red from the round paddle the man standing behind her kept wielding with skin-smacking force.

Skye's smile held a hint of envy, adding to Mickie's confusion. "That's Kathie, and she likes it longer and harder than most, and goes out of her way to irritate her Dom into delivering. That's Master Neil, who's usually easygoing until she pushes him too far. But don't knock the merits of a spanking until you've laid over a Dom's lap. I did, but my Clayton showed me how a little pain could notch up the heat in an effective way. How about a drink?"

Mickie would take her word for it since she didn't plan on going there with anyone. She'd likely haul off and smack the guy or laugh at the absurdity of finding herself in the ridiculous position at her age. "I could use one," she replied, going with her to the bar along the left side. "You look familiar. Did you grow up here?"

"No, I've only been here since last summer, not even a year. Do you read much? I'm..."

"S.L. Anders!" Mickie exclaimed, clicking her fingers as she made the connection. "I heard you lived here now and remember seeing your picture at the library."

Settling on a barstool, Skye's grin turned rueful. "I wish they'd take that down. I've asked them to several times. Hey, Master Nick, this is our guest tonight, Mickie Taylor."

"Mickie, welcome to Spurs." He surprised her by holding out a hand across the bar, just like any polite gentleman instead of a dominant bully.

"Thank you. Nice to meet you." With his Stetson shielding his eyes she couldn't make out the color, but she could feel the potency of his gaze through her thin top. His tanned face, chiseled jaw, and crisp, curly black chest hair revealed by his open vest were enough to dampen her panties.

"What can I get you ladies?" he asked, his mouth curling with a hint of amusement, as if he knew the impact he had on her.

Mickie refused to look away as she replied, "I'll take a beer, please."

"Screwdriver for me," Skye said before turning to Mickie as Nick moved away. "Don't worry, all the guys here have that effect on us."

"Am I that obvious?" If so, that would be a first for her. She'd found other men attractive at first sight before, but none had caused an instant, physical reaction. Something else for her to examine later.

"Only to someone who's been there. Clayton is monitoring, so I have about an hour. Would you like a tour, or would you rather grab a table and visit? My friends Lisa and Poppy are with their Dom husbands, but we can join Jen, who's sitting with Charlotte."

Pivoting on the stool, Mickie looked at the pair Skye indicated, recognizing the owner of the Miner's Junction B&B from high school. "I remember Jen, but doubt she'll know me."

"You never know." Master Nick returned with their drinks and handed them over. "Thank you, Sir," Skye said.

Nick nodded then looked at Mickie as she reached for the frosted glass. Even though it grated to do so, she followed Skye's example and reiterated her response. "Thank you, Sir."

His lips quirked. "There, that wasn't so hard, was it?" Before she could question his astute, correct reading of her, he dipped his head. "Enjoy your evening," he stated before moving down the bar to assist someone else.

Two other men came up to the bar, nodded in polite greeting but otherwise ignored them as they took a seat. Mickie didn't know whether she was relieved or irked no one tried to engage her in conversation or proposition her into trying a scene.

Glancing her way, Skye laughed. "All the Doms read your guest application, so they're aware you're only interested in socializing and observing, just in case you're wondering."

"I know I'm not a walking sex bomb," she returned dryly. "And I dressed to deflect attention but do appreciate knowing that."

"It's taken me a while, but this isn't always about sex. For some, their needs run down different paths, and our guys are diverse enough with their own desires to meet the needs of just about anyone. They could range from a bout of uncomplicated sex as a way to wind down from a busy week to helping someone break through a mental block or deal with an emotional crisis when traditional help has failed. Believe it or not, there are merits to putting yourself into someone else's hands. It can be freeing to let go without having to make any decisions or fret over what you're doing."

So much to think about and consider. Mickie eyed the woman with her arms bound above her head, wrists attached to cuffs at the end of a dangling chain. She was naked and blindfolded, the man holding a wicked looking, multi-strand whip in one hand and caressing her pink-striped breasts with the other gazing at her with an intent expression Mickie couldn't define. She shivered, unable to imagine trusting one of these strangers enough to give them that much control over her, or render herself to such a vulnerable position. The only person she'd ever been close enough to and would trust with her life was Randy, and picturing herself on the chain in front of him sent a wave of shocking heat coursing through her bloodstream to pool between her legs.

Fudge. Thinking along those lines would not do, and besides, since Randy was not around and she wouldn't let her wishful thinking return down that path, her interest remained the same – nonexistent regarding the kink.

"Mickie Taylor, it's great to see you again," Jen said as they approached their table.

Nothing could have warmed her more than that simple acknowledgement of remembrance. She'd been a nobody growing up, Chelsea her only close friend, and hadn't cared, especially once she'd met Randy. Jen was two years older, and that she'd noticed her back then enough to remember her came as a pleasant surprise.

"Hi, Jen. It's been a long time," she returned, taking a seat.

"Too long. This is Charlotte. What brings you out here tonight?"

Mickie smiled at Charlotte, trying not to ogle the way her busty chest was displayed in a tight, white corset that displayed her abundant flesh. She wanted to kick herself when she turned self-conscious over her smaller size.

"Heck if I know," she replied honestly, with a rueful twist of her lips. "I thought to get out and socialize as well as satisfy my curiosity about the place. It's not what I imagined, and yet it is, which doesn't make a lick of sense."

All three of them chuckled. "More than you know," Charlotte said. Looking down at her breasts, she admitted, "On my first night, never in a million years did I think I would be sitting here like this someday. Now I love it, this place, the people here, and the benefits I reap from the Doms who know me. Two years ago, I experienced your same reaction and thoughts as a guest."

Jen cocked her head, picking up her glass. "I

heard somewhere you've taken over as foreman on the Daniels' ranch. Does that mean you're back to stay?"

Mickie shrugged and took a swallow of beer before answering. "I haven't decided yet. A lot depends on my dad since my mom has packed up and left."

"I'm sorry." Skye squeezed her hand. "I lost my mother last summer and still miss her."

"Well, I don't miss my mom. Tell me about that contraption." She pointed with her beer bottle toward the funny-looking wood cross, ready to change the subject.

Thankfully, they took the cue and talk turned to the different apparatus around the room, each of them relating details of their scenes on them. Mickie learned as much from their open revelations as she did the different inflections in their voices, ranging from lustful sighs of ecstasy to soft wonderment of contentment they said they hadn't found anywhere else.

By the time she left, Mickie had a new respect for those who enjoyed the lifestyle and new friends she hoped to get to know better. Between meeting everyone tonight and her job, she figured she could be happy again here even without Randy around.

****

It was after midnight when Randy pulled into the garage of the house he'd built on a few acres from his parents, the one he'd lived in with Melanie. He didn't get the painful twist in his gut this time, and, as he entered and flipped on a light in the kitchen, he didn't automatically picture her in there wearing nothing but an apron and a smile. Submissive to the bone, there'd been a time he'd thought she was perfect for him. A year after learning of her infidelity, he could finally admit what they'd had was superficial, a solvent for baser needs that could have been met by any deeply submissive woman. He had no idea what he wanted in a relationship going forward, only that he didn't want a repeat of his failed marriage.

Exhaustion tugged at him, and he left his bags in the truck for morning. His parents planned on leaving then but not early. He still couldn't believe old man Sanders agreed to take off for a month with them. Miss Betty must have a bigger influence on him than he'd imagined. A lot had changed in the year he'd stayed away. One of the three men he had sold Spurs to, Dakota, was the least likely to settle down with one woman, or so everyone had thought. Shawn and Clayton were also married, and his mother passed on recently that Ben Wilkins was planning on getting hitched.

Turning off the light, he made his way to his bedroom in the dark, stripped, and dropped onto his king-size bed. As he fell asleep, he found himself looking forward to being home for the first time in way too long.

Randy took a quick shower, ate a granola bar for breakfast, and poured his coffee into an insulated mug with a lid to take with him as he left the house the next morning. He welcomed the warm but cooler summer air compared to the Texas sweltering heat. Opting to walk the distance between his house and the ranch buildings, he went over what he'd like to do today. Meeting the new foreman would have to wait until Monday since she had weekends off, but he could touch base with the guys, get a feel for her through them before taking Cheyenne or Black Jack out for a run.

As he came over the rise and the stable came into view, he spotted a familiar truck parked in front, and his pulse jumped with the unexpected pleasure of seeing Mickie again today. He'd planned on looking her up in the next few days but couldn't be more pleased to start the day catching up with her. Entering the stable, he followed her frustrated mutterings echoing from the tack room, grinning when he got close enough to make out her words.

"Well, *fudge*, get in there, would ya?"

Reaching the door, he paused, eyeing her long legs and nicely rounded ass in snug jeans from her bent over position on a sawhorse. He was shocked when his body stirred with a frisson of heated lust. He hadn't thought of her as a kid for years, but this was the first time he'd regarded her as a desirable woman. Tamping down the unaccustomed response he needed time to assimilate, he leaned against the doorjamb and drawled, "Something giving you a tough time, Mickie?"

Mickie whirled around, surprised pleasure flushing her face before a familiar look of suspicion darkened her eyes to pewter, the quick change amusing him.

"What are you doing here, Randy?" She reached for a rag on the workbench behind her and wiped at her grease-stained hands, never taking her eyes off him.

"Last time I checked, I still live here." Walking forward, he held out his cup. "Need a pick-me-up?"

"Thanks." She took a few sips then handed it back. "Are you here to see your parents before they leave?"

Growing annoyed with her cool reception while he was struggling to keep from picturing her bent over that sawhorse again, only this time with those tight jeans shoved down to her knees, he clenched his hands so he wouldn't touch her until he got himself under control. He was so stunned by this unexpected change toward the girl he'd known for so long, he couldn't risk alienating her by reaching for her with an intent he wasn't sure of and would likely drive her away.

"Yes, but I'm staying this time, Mickie." When she stiffened at that, a light bulb went off in his head, and he put two and two together. "You're our new foreman." And his mother had some answering to do.

Her eyes flashed, and her mouth set in a familiar belligerent slash. "Yes, and I don't intend to give up this job just because you've finally decided to stick around again. Your parents hired me. They'll have to fire me if you're taking over."

Randy could see the worry and anger swirling in her stormy gaze and the hurt she was trying to hide behind those emotions. Mickie had always been insecure over certain things, but he'd never been one of them. She covered her hurt feelings with attitude, and his heart turned over as he wondered why she would think so low of him. Stifling the urge to loosen her tight lips with the pressure of his, he set the coffee cup on a shelf to his right and moved with slow stealth and purpose toward her. He didn't stop until he'd backed her against the wall of hanging tack and braced his hands against it behind her, caging her in as he pressed close.

"I'm not taking over, and that you would believe either I or my parents would act in such a way toward anyone, let alone you, is unjustified and irritating as hell. I will take Dad's place overseeing our ranch and keeping the books, and I'll do my share of the work, just as I did before I left. You will still have the duties and responsibilities and dad entrusted you with, and I'll go over those with them before they leave. In fact, I insist you come up to the house with me to talk then see them off. You can tell me why you're here, working on your day off."

Blowing out a breath that wafted in a warm caress against his throat, she shrugged her shoulders as if his order were no big deal. "Sure. I planned to tell them goodbye anyway. And I'm sorry. I'm having a bad day, is all."

Since she wasn't pushing him away or insisting he back off, he remained close to her, liking the heat from her body seeping into his, the spark in those silver eyes that revealed an awareness of him as more than a longtime friend and big brother figure, even though he was sure she would deny it. He was still working his way around this new attraction to her. The strong-willed and oftentimes annoying kid was still there, but so was a woman he wanted in a way he'd never dreamed possible between him and her.

"You're forgiven, naturally. Want to tell me about it?" he asked, reaching down to take her hand and tug her from the room. He was pleased when her fingers curled around his.

She huffed but answered, "My dad was at his worst this morning, is all. You'd think I would be used to his complaints, wouldn't you?"

He turned to her as they stepped outside, anger on her behalf coiling through his gut, the same reaction he always experienced when she would show up upset over her parents' constant arguing. "No, you shouldn't be, and you shouldn't have to put up with his attitude when, I'm guessing, you've been helping him out with your mother gone."

Mickie looked away from him, blinking like she always did when she was fighting tears or showing gratitude for support. He'd never seen her cry, not even when she was so young and neglected by her irresponsible, self-centered parents. Her brick wall of independence stemmed from having to fend for herself at an early age, and she used it as a shield to keep from getting close to anyone, including him. If, after a bout of soul searching, he decided to pursue a different relationship with her, breaking through that barrier wouldn't be easy.

Shaking her head, she tossed him a quick, grateful look. "Thanks for understanding."

"Don't I always?" he asked, resuming walking up to the house.

Mickie snorted, replying with a bite of sarcasm. "No, you can be as obtuse as all men."

"What's that supposed to mean?"

"Nothing," she answered, rolling her eyes.

"Huh, that statement usually means the opposite. We can discuss it when we go riding this afternoon." Randy gazed down at her as he held open the front door, catching the excitement on her face before she narrowed her eyes up at him.

"There's nothing more to discuss on that subject. Don't you have some bimbo waiting to do your bidding today?"

"Jealous?" He couldn't help teasing her.

"Not hardly," Mickie drawled, her eyes lit with humor. "Hey, if that's your type, at least this time around, find someone who's smart enough not to look elsewhere while she has you." She winced, entering the house ahead of him. "Sorry. I didn't mean to bring up a bad memory or touchy subject."

"The end of my marriage is neither of those things anymore. It took me a while, but I finally wised up. Did you just pay me a compliment? If so, it has to be a first, and thanks."

"If I did, it was by mistake," she retorted with a smile.

"I'll take it anyway." *And you, any way I can get you I'm beginning to think.*

That thought ought to disturb him considering before today he'd never imagined Mickie playing any role in his life other than a kid he'd befriended and taken under his wing and given a chance to escape her troublesome home life when she'd needed it most. But it didn't unsettle or confuse him. In fact, the more he considered the idea, the more it seemed...right in a way he couldn't explain.

As a sizzle of anticipation went through him, Randy thought his return home was looking up in more ways than one.

Chapter Five

The slow stretch of Randy's chiseled lips hit Mickie with a gut-wrenching sucker punch as warmth encircled her heart, the same response she'd experienced when she saw him again in the stable without any warning. *No, no, no*, she lamented, resisting the urge to turn and bang her head against the wall. That reaction would not do. She'd stayed away so long to get over him, praying with endless regularity for a much less potent reaction to his presence ever since overhearing him describe her as nothing more than an adopted family member to Melanie. Disappointment swamped her upon learning those pleas had gone unanswered. Given she'd convinced herself she'd put this ridiculous, one-sided infatuation to bed once and for all, her response didn't bode well for achieving that goal anytime soon.

I can do this, remain his friend and do my

job, she continued to lecture herself. *Easy. Piece of cake.* If only he hadn't pressed his tall, muscled body so close to hers, and if she couldn't still swear he'd looked at her with lust in those chocolate eyes. With his Stetson tipped low, she couldn't be sure, and it didn't matter if she'd read him right or was mixing up her own heated vibes to his nearness with his look. She refused to let herself go in that direction again now that she was older and wiser.

"There you are, dear, and Mickie, too. You didn't have to take time from your day off to come by, dear, but I'm glad you did," Caroline said, coming into the foyer with a beaming smile.

Mickie braced herself for Caroline's hug, still unused to such open displays of affection, even after all these years. Someday, she promised herself, she would learn to let go and accept they cared without expecting a reversal of their feelings toward her at any given time.

"You two have a fun time and take lots of pictures," she said, returning her embrace before stepping back and bumping into Randy.

A different stiffness tightened her muscles upon coming into contact with his hard body again, her buttocks clenching with the brief press of his groin against her softer flesh. Moving aside, she grew suspicious when his hand landed on her shoulder and his mother noticed with a twinkle in her eyes.

Shrugging off the possessive hold, she flicked him a censuring glare before telling Caroline, "Maybe someday I'll have the chance to travel south and visit New Orleans and a beach."

"Of course you will." Caroline hugged Randy. "You were supposed to let us know when you got in."

"It was late, which is why I called you earlier. Are you packed and ready?"

"Yes, we are, so let's get going, Caro," Ron replied, joining them and giving Randy a guy hug. "Glad to have you back, Son, but not enough to delay our departure. We don't want to give Sanders time to change his mind. Betty would never forgive us."

"You probably have that right." Randy sent Mickie a small smile but addressed his parents as he said, "Funny how neither of you mentioned you hired our Mickie to take over for Steven."

Caroline waved an airy hand, turning away from him. "It must have slipped my mind. I'm ready, Ron. We'll catch up more when we return."

Mickie walked out with them but let Randy see them off without her. Lifting her hand in a farewell gesture, she started back to the stables, way too pleased when he caught up with her and slung a muscular arm around her shoulders.

"Let's take that ride, and you can tell me why you canceled on me the last time I saw you."

"Don't you forget anything?" she grumbled, not wanting to discuss his ex with him.

"Not anything to do with you, it seems," he returned without any sign of awkwardness over that admission.

She didn't know what to make of his open declaration, so she let it go as they approached the stable. "I should get going, let you settle in. Toby is working today."

Randy halted and nudged his hat back, pinning her with the censoring look in his direct, dark gaze. "I've never known you to run away from something you're uncomfortable with instead of facing it head on."

Bristling, she fisted her hands on her hips and returned his cool glare. "What are you talking about?"

"This." He reached out a hand, cupped her nape, and hauled her up against him, wrapping his other arm around her waist. "You don't know what to make of this change in me toward you. Well, guess what, Mickie, I don't either."

The soft brush of his lips over hers shook

Mickie, the slight pressure so different from the quick smacks he'd always given her before. There was a time she believed this was what she wanted from him, but no more, no matter that slight contact burned through her bloodstream.

She opened her mouth to tell him she didn't want this but instead found herself saying, "I thought you wanted to go for a ride."

Raising one dark eyebrow, he drawled with a suggestiveness that tickled her throat with a bubble of laughter, "Oh, I do, Mickie, fast and hard or slow and easy, however you wish to go."

"You're bad," she teased back, unable to resist him in such a playful mood. "Save it for one of those women eager to kowtow to your demands. Black Jack and I will race you and Cheyenne and leave you in the dust."

She took off toward the rear paddock with a laugh. Only Randy could irritate her one minute and make her laugh in the next. That didn't mean she would let him push her into changing their relationship, regardless of the way her body kept clamoring for his possession.

Randy followed Mickie, accepting the challenge she tossed out and the one she wasn't aware she issued with that remark about other women. Maybe he just wanted something or someone different enough from his wife and their lifestyle to ensure he wouldn't make such a mistake again in choosing the wrong partner. Either that, or the girl he held a deep fondness for meant much more to him than that. A return to the club he used to own should give him the answer to this surprising turn of events today. If he managed a spark of interest tonight at Spurs toward one of the submissive members, he could believe Mickie's sudden appeal on a whole different level than he was used to was a fluke from not seeing her in so long.

Like countless times over the years, he watched her heft a saddle onto Black Jack without a strain, her toned arms as strong as those slender legs he kept fantasizing wrapped around his hips or shoulders. As she put one booted foot in the stirrup, he couldn't resist reaching out and giving her a boost with a hand on her butt. He wasn't disappointed when she scowled down at him as soon as she sat astride the stallion.

"I've been mounting a horse, this horse, for years without assistance."

"Are you flushed because I helped you when you didn't need it or for another reason?" he taunted, cocking his head. He did enjoy sparring with her.

Sucking in a deep breath, her hands tightened on the reins. "Just mount up if you still want to go."

"Oh, I still want to go, Mickie."

Those silver eyes flashed, and she yanked on the reins, turning Black Jack then kicking him into a trot out the gate without another word. Chuckling, Randy hurried to catch up with her. As soon as they were side by side, she tossed him a grin, her pique obviously set aside for the fun of a race.

"Ready?"

Without waiting for him to answer, she took off across the pasture, her long braid flying out behind her, her laugh echoing on the wind. That daredevil attitude caused a familiar clutch of worry in his gut, and he nudged Cheyenne into a run even though there was no reason for him to fret. She'd taken her share of tumbles when first learning to ride, but those bruises hadn't deterred her from becoming an excellent horsewoman. Old habits though were hard to break, and he doubted the protectiveness that started the day they met would ever stop.

Randy let her reach their large pond nestled at the base of a mountain ridge first, enjoying the wide grin of triumph she tossed him as much as the flare of annoyance that replaced it when he said, "I let you win, you know."

"Did not," she returned hotly.

Shaking his head at her stubborn competitive streak, he nudged Cheyenne to the edge of the bank and relaxed the reins so he could drink alongside Black Jack. "I know the futility of arguing with you, so I won't bother. What are your plans for the rest of the day?"

Mickie's slender shoulders slumped, her gaze shifting to the distant view of mountains. "I need to help my dad with a few things."

Reaching over, he palmed her chin and turned her to face him. "Even though I admire your loyalty, you don't owe him anything. He's an adult and can take care of himself."

"Yeah, I keep telling myself that, but it doesn't stick when he guilts me with his complaining." She pulled away from his hold and tugged on her reins. "Let's head back. I'm sure you have a lot to catch up on."

He did, and one was figuring out why, after all these years he found himself craving that toned, tight body in a way that would likely shock her as much as him. The first thing he intended to do when she left was call one of the friends he had sold Spurs to and inquire about visiting tonight. They might find his return to the place he sold them awkward, but as much as he wouldn't mind owning a piece of the club again, he would never put them in an uncomfortable position by asking for his property back.

They returned to the stable at a slower pace, catching up with each other on the ride back. Randy heard the fondness Mickie had for the veterinarian she worked for in Colorado in her voice, and the love of her work. As they dismounted at the corral, he looked at her over Cheyenne's back, his respect for her decision to put her own life on hold while she helped her neglectful, lazy-assed father adjust to her mother's deflection rising to a new level.

"Don't put up with any crap from your old man, Mickie. You deserve better than that."

Tugging the saddle off her horse, she shook her head. "Maybe, maybe not. He's going through a rough time, but don't worry. I know where to draw the line."

Her eyes clouded over, as if she were remembering something unpleasant, and he grew suspicious. Taylor might have already come close to crossing that line. "Make sure you stick to that, or come to me. I'll be happy to set him straight."

Mickie turned Black Jack out to the pasture

then stopped in front of him. "Thanks, Randy, but that won't be necessary." She started to lift her hand then dropped it to her side. "I'm glad you're back. See you on Monday."

Watching her hightail it to her truck, Randy resisted the temptation to snatch her against him again, this time giving her a longer, deeper kiss, exploring her stubborn mouth until she melted in his arms. Ridiculous, of course, since there was no way in hell the attitude-riddled girl he knew so well would ever respond to his dominance the same as the submissive women he'd enjoyed in the past.

He sure hoped one of those submissives stirred him as much, or more, tonight, thus proving the need gripping his balls in a tight fist was nothing but a strange fluke following their longest separation.

****

Mickie drove back to the trailer park vowing there was no way Randy's return or the resurrection of her longing to jump his thickly muscled bones would keep her from returning to Spurs tonight. She not only needed the distraction of socializing with her new friends again, but she wouldn't allow hormones to dictate her life. Since he was no longer owner of the club, she assumed he wouldn't welcome the idea of joining as a member. Maybe his wife's infidelity had soured him on that whole lifestyle, her cheating proof she wasn't the submissive he'd thought she was or that he desired.

She breathed a sigh of relief when she saw her dad's car gone as she pulled in front of the trailer. With him out, she could get the place cleaned up and his dinner fixed without listening to his harping about her mother's desertion and Mickie's job that kept her away all day. If only she could get him interested in something, anything except griping about his life. Someday, she mused, she might get through to him, like when pigs fly.

He came in several hours later, right as she was leaving, scowling in displeasure when he took in the sundress and heels she wore. "Where the hell you off to this time, girl?" he growled, shoving past her.

She could smell the alcohol on him, proof he'd spent the afternoon at the bar. "I'm going out. Your dinner is in the oven. I suggest you eat and sleep it off." Opening the door, she slammed out, ignoring his cursing, glad to get away until he was in bed. The last thing she needed tonight, while still struggling with her reaction to Randy's return, was to deal with one of her dad's drunken rantings. The sober ones were bad enough.

The parking lot was as crowded tonight as last night, and she took a moment after parking to run nervous hands down her sides. She rarely wore dresses, but after Dakota Smith approved her guest pass for another night, he informed her she would have to adhere to their dress code tonight. The online description of the club's rules regarding clothing were simple – anything that left a lot of skin bare. The rule rubbed her wrong, as she didn't plan on participating any more tonight than last night, but she stifled her vexation for the opportunity to have a place to hang out with people she liked being around as opposed to spending the evening at home.

A frisson of excitement spread through Mickie when she entered the foyer and the seductive beat of a song she didn't know seeped through the door to the main room. Since heels were the only shoes allowed, she left hers on and opened the interior door, recognizing Charlotte standing at the sign-in podium.

"Hey there, Mickie. I was glad to see your name on the list again." The brunette greeted her with a smile, appearing at ease in her baby doll, see-through nightie that revealed her full breasts.

Mickie had never given her small chest much thought until coming here. But, as another wave of self-consciousness gripped her, she tensed with exasperation, having no use for such an emotion over her physical attributes.

"Thanks, Charlotte. It was fun hanging out last night." She signed her name, scanning the room for more familiar faces, recognizing the sheriff's wife, Lisa, sitting with a redhead and Skye at a table. She hadn't met either woman but had seen the sheriff with his new wife a few times when in town.

Skye waved her over as Charlotte said, "Go on. They've been watching for you. I'm ready to catch a Dom's attention."

She almost envied the younger girl's enthusiasm and unabashed need for a dominant member's attention. Almost.

Three men leaning against the bar shifted their attention toward Mickie as she walked over to join Skye and the others, tempting her to tug on the short, mid-thigh length of her dress. She wasn't a prude and had enjoyed several affairs over the past few years, but something about these male looks sent shivers of awareness down her spine and warm pulses between her legs without them getting near her or touching her. Odd, disconcerting, and yeah, arousing she was willing to admit only to herself.

Lisa's green gaze turned knowing as Mickie

took a seat at their table. "Don't worry, we've all experienced that reaction to this place, and questioned our sanity at first. I'm Lisa McDuff."

"Mickie Taylor, and good. Misery does love company. Nice to meet you." Mickie held out a hand to the redhead. "I'm the new kid on the block."

"Been there recently. Poppy Smith." She jerked a thumb toward the tall man dressed in black, leaning against the wall. His huge arms were crossed, his eyes shielded by his lowered Stetson, yet Mickie could still sense his acute attention. "That's Dakota, my husband."

The big man's tall, dark looks matched the tone Mickie got from him in their brief online exchange. "He's the one who answered my request to return and gave me instructions on abiding by the dress code tonight. Seeing him, I'm glad I didn't give in to the temptation to argue with his bossy tone."

Skye giggled. "Poppy is the only one who can get away with talking back to Master Dakota. It's fun to watch."

"Yeah, because you're not earning one of his punishments," Poppy returned dryly.

"Don't act like that bothers you," Lisa chided. "The last time you were lying over his lap, I watched you orgasm as he spanked you with the wooden paddle."

"Not my fault. He used his fingers at the same time." Poppy flicked a heated glance at her husband, who returned it with a curl of his lips that spoke volumes.

Mickie got a kick out of their bantering back and forth, willing the stab of envy jabbing her over the close bond the three of them seemed to share to go away. She didn't understand their pleasure in pain but wondered if she could accept parts of this lifestyle if it meant enjoying such a special relationship.

Randy's face popped into her head, her body's instant reaction to the press of his in the tack room, the burn from the brief caress of his mouth against hers returning to taunt her. Just thinking about him touching her with his large, calloused hands and fingers sent need coursing through her bloodstream, alarming her with the intensity.

"Excuse me," she said, pushing back from the table. "I'm going to get a drink and use the restroom."

The three men were still there as she went up to the bar, one nodding and giving her a small smile that helped ease the tenseness in her shoulders. She warmed again from their gazes but nothing that compared to what went through her when she thought of getting close to Randy again. She came tonight, in part, to get away from these new and unwanted feelings, but, so far, nothing was working, damn it.

The man closest to her held out his hand. "Nice to have you back again, Mickie. I'm sorry I didn't get a chance to meet you last night. I'm Master Neil."

She returned his handshake, liking the twinkle in his blue eyes and the way his black hair curled around his tanned neck, but she also remembered his dark expression when she'd seen him using the paddle on Kathie last night. "Thank you...Sir," she added after the bald man sporting a gold loop earring standing next to him narrowed his dark eyes in warning.

Master Nick, the third man, slapped him on the back. "Ease up, Simon. She's new."

Simon came around Neil and squeezed her shoulder. "Welcome, Mickie," was all he said before striding away.

Something about that one caused a ripple of unease under Mickie's skin, but she shoved it aside when the sheriff joined them from behind the bar.

"Mickie Taylor, it's been a while. Master Dakota mentioned you were returning, and I'm glad I got to see you tonight. Can I get you something?"

"I'll have a beer, thank you, Sheriff. I met your wife. Congratulations."

His gray eyes lifted over her head, and she watched his mouth soften as he looked at Lisa before nodding to Mickie. "I appreciate that. How is your dad?"

"He's struggling dealing with the divorce, but otherwise the same."

He reached out and patted her hand. Shawn McDuff had always treated her with respect, showing an interest in her and her welfare when she was younger and still living at home. Most people in Mountain Bend were just as friendly and caring, but there were always those who were jackasses, and she'd been called white trash and ridiculed in school by more than one cruel adolescent. Those taunts had ended when she'd started hanging out at the Daniels ranch, and she always suspected Randy might have said something to those boys.

"You call my office if you need anything. I'll get your drink."

"I'll be right back. Thanks." She made her way back out to the foyer feeling eyes on her again, unused to such focused attention. The restrooms were in the short hall off the foyer, and she took her time dabbing her heated face with cold water and working to get thoughts of Randy out of her head before returning. That lasted until she opened the door into the club room again and he was the first person she saw, leaning with negligent ease on the bar top, the short sleeves of his khaki dress shirt stretched tight across his broad shoulders, chest, and bulging arms.

Mickie's throat went dry when her first thought went right to wondering if his scruffy jawline would scratch her cheek when he kissed her, or if the short bristles were soft. She threw her shoulders back in stiff irritation, cursing herself for her inability to get this sudden weakness for him under control. Then he saw her, and the heat of his gaze penetrated the distance between them, and she went damp.

Just like that.

Fudge.

Randy's words died in his throat when he glanced up, and shock gripped him by the balls at seeing Mickie enter from the foyer. The last person he expected to see tonight, or in Spurs at all, was her, but the instant pleasure sweeping through him proved he wasn't opposed even though he couldn't imagine her fitting in here. He'd never seen her hair loose, and she looked pretty with the long red-tinted blonde tresses hanging down. Another first, and one that sent a hot wave of lust through him, was eyeing that well-toned, slender body encased in a short, clinging sheath, looking fucking sexy in heels that drew the eyes to her long, shapely legs.

Damn, Mickie had grown up right under his nose and cleaned up way too nice. A surge of possessive lust hit him when he noticed the appreciative gazes turned her way. Of course, he wasn't about to reveal any of his surprising reactions to her presence here. He didn't have a death wish, just a new Mickie wish he'd thought coming here could squash.

Randy accepted then embraced the instant, edgy need snaking through him, slithering through his bloodstream with hot, greedy lust, hardening him into a voracious hunger. For Mickie, the kid he'd always looked upon as a younger sister and, on too many occasions, a thorn in his side. For two decades, he'd harbored a fondness for her, but not once in all those years before today, had he looked at her with anything in mind except protective caring.

Shawn had just surprised him by asking if he'd like to buy into the club and become a joint owner. The excitement and pleasure of that unexpected offer took a back seat to wondering what the hell had instigated this visit since there was no way Mickie would submit to any of these Doms.

"I forgot you two are well acquainted," Shawn drawled, leaning his forearms on the bar top.

"Apparently not well enough, unless she's undergone a drastic change since I saw her last." Mickie started toward him, her slender body tense, the look in her eyes unreadable for a change. "How long has she been a member?"

"She's not yet. Last night was her first visit, and all she wants to do is hang out. She didn't even tour the place, just sat with some of the women and visited, from what I saw."

"*Mmmm*, I think I need to have a talk with her," Randy murmured, unable to take his eyes off those soft yet strong legs as she approached.

"Good luck with that," Shawn returned, his tone amused.

"I have a feeling I'll need it."

Randy let Mickie speak first when she reached the bar, her eyes wary, a rare blush staining her cheeks. Was she uncomfortable with his presence and him finding her here or because he didn't bother hiding he wanted more from her than friendship?

"I thought you gave this place up," she said, her voice carrying a hint of accusation as she reached for the beer Shawn handed over.

"And I never imagined you setting foot inside. I guess we were both mistaken. Come with me." He snatched her hand as she stepped back, drank the last of his whiskey, and set the glass down before straightening. "Thanks, Shawn. I'll get back with you and the guys on your offer."

"No rush."

"Where are you taking me?" Mickie demanded as he tugged on her hand, the breathless catch in her voice telling.

"Over here for some privacy, for starters." Leading her into the three-sided, semi-secluded alcove created by stacked haybales in the corner, he settled on the wide armchair and pulled her onto his lap. He needed answers, sooner rather than later. "Sit still," he commanded when she struggled to free herself from the arm he wrapped around her waist.

She went rigid and glared at him. "Don't talk to me in that tone. I'm not…"

"As long as we're here, I'm the Dom, and you'll behave accordingly, or we can leave to have this conversation. Your call." He knew she would take that ultimatum as a challenge.

She lifted her stubborn chin. "I'm not running away from either you or this place. What do you want?"

Randy released her hand and, unable to resist, placed his palm on the inside of her thigh, halfway between knee and groin. Her blush deepened, her eyes darkening as her muscles tensed under him. He gave her a slow smile, pleased with her response to his touch even though she wasn't.

"Why did I never know how soft your skin is or notice your well-shaped legs before now?"

Mickie fidgeted, the uncomfortable awareness etched on her face making her defensive. "How am I supposed to know?" she snapped. "What is going on with you?"

"Hell if I know, Mickie." He sighed and squeezed her thigh. She sucked in a deep breath that lifted her chest. "Now, you tell me what your interest is in coming here. I can't believe you've changed that much since I saw you last."

She tossed her head, and her loose hair tickled his arm. "Maybe I have. You've been gone a long time."

Randy narrowed his eyes. She always went on the defensive when she was uncomfortable with a truth about herself. Question was, was she realizing an interest in the lifestyle or in him?

Chapter Six

Mickie couldn't look away from Randy's dark, compelling gaze as he replied, "Not that long."

How could she concentrate on getting back on track with her reason for being here when she couldn't keep her mind out of the gutter? Randy had touched her countless times over the years, but none of those innocent contacts had torched her skin the way his hand on her thigh did. She'd certainly never sat on his lap or felt the press of his erection against her butt before, or imagined she would respond to both with a damp heat filling her pussy.

"I get it. You were heartbroken and needed time away to heal, but that doesn't mean..." She paused on a gasp as he leaned forward and nipped her lower lip, shocked when her nipples puckered in reaction to the minor sting.

"I'm beginning to rethink my reasoning about my marriage, and other things. Tell me why you're here."

Because she really wanted to question him about that, she shoved her curiosity aside and tried to think of a way to deter him from the path he seemed to want to go down, for whatever reason. It was one she'd wanted to travel with him long ago and thought she'd gotten over that ridiculous idea. Obviously not, if she went by the rapid flow of her blood to her pussy the moment she saw him.

"I'm curious, is all. So many people seem to enjoy this place, and I needed to get out."

"I can buy you needed a diversion from your dad but not that you're curious about this lifestyle. Try again."

Mickie bristled at his astuteness and gripped his wrist to shove his hand off her leg, but he just dug his fingers in tighter. "Knock it off. If you don't believe me, let me go and find someone else to pester."

Instead of backing down, he narrowed his eyes with a familiar look of exasperation. "Look, it appears we're headed for a change in our relationship, and it's best we deal with the intimacy that poses with open honesty."

"What are you talking about?" She knew, but her head kept arguing with her body not to go there.

To cover that dilemma, she scoffed, rolling her eyes. "An affair? I never said I was interested in going there with you."

His gaze turned smug. "You didn't have to; your body has said it for you."

Before she could stop him, he slid his hand up her thigh and under her dress to trace his fingers over her damp panties, dipping his head for a quick tug on one nipple. Even through her clothing, her body went berserk, throbbing with an undeniable ache for more.

Lifting his head, he stayed focused on her face, pressing one finger between her pussy lips, pushing her silk panties between her labia. "Your body doesn't lie as easily as your mouth. Any fabrications from you going forward will be met with retribution. Remember that."

"For God's sake, Randy!" she burst out, baffled by the surge of heated dampness that threat produced. "You can't expect me to kneel at your feet and start calling you Sir twenty-four seven."

A stern look came over his face, one she'd never seen directed at her. With an unexpected pinch to her nipple that confused her even more when she couldn't separate the discomfort from the stab of pleasure, he said, "I'm going into this not expecting or asking you to change, willing to make adjustments for that prickly, independent side of you to a certain point. You will have to do the same. When it comes to sex, I'm Master Randy, and you'll show respect here, at least. And no, I won't insist you kneel at my feet unless I want your mouth on me and that's the best position for where we're at. Understood?"

No, not at all. Not my sudden desire to explore this side of you or my responses so far to being here with you. Still, she decided, the best way to get rid of an itch was to scratch it, and maybe agreeing to his suggestion was the fastest way to put this all to bed, so to speak, for both of them.

"Say I agree to give this a try. Are you going to go all caveman on me when I fail to meet your requirements? I'm not Melanie or any of these other submissive women," she felt compelled to point out.

Mickie couldn't read his expression when he turned thoughtful, but she recognized his rueful smile and relaxed. "I'm well aware you're nothing like them, and no, I won't do anything you can't say no to using a safeword. The best way to see if any of this lifestyle is for you is by trial and error, and I sure as hell am not about to let someone else tutor you. You're normally a 'jump right in' person when trying something new. Do you want to be that venturesome and go out there for a demonstration?" He jerked his head toward the opening to the nook. "Or play it safe and stay here, in private?"

She tensed again, not liking the way he phrased her choices, issuing a challenge he knew she wouldn't turn from. "Why delay the inevitable? Just remember, *Master* Randy, I have ways of getting even."

"I look forward to you trying. Let's go."

Sliding his hand out from under her dress, he nudged her up and took her hand, the snug grip of his damp fingers a welcome reassurance she would never admit needing. The milling crowd, stimulating beat resonating in the background, and the row of apparatus he led her toward all took on a new meaning now that she'd agreed to go out on a limb she'd sworn held no appeal for her. Was it the thought of public exposure, her determination to see this through, or Randy's touch and the way he kept her close that was responsible for the rush of arousing excitement teasing her senses? She supposed the next thirty minutes would yield an answer, and they would either put this idea of an affair behind them or embark on a short detour from their usual relationship.

Mickie went hot with embarrassment when

Randy paused by a naked woman whose arms were strapped down on the arm rests of a chair tilted back, her legs spread, thighs and ankles bound, rendering her unable to move. Master Simon, the Dom showing a harder edge than most, snapped a small wood slapper on one nipple, leaving the puckered bud a bright red. Wincing, she couldn't deny the woman's obvious pleasure from that painful swat as evidenced by the glistening sheen coating her exposed slit.

Randy gazed down at her and winked. "Relax. You're a long way from anything like this."

"Like in never." *No way, no how.*

Resuming walking, he said, "Never say never, Mickie." He halted between two unoccupied contraptions. "You choose, a chain or a bench?"

Cocking her head, she examined each and decided the chain would allow for an easier release when she called a halt. He had to know she wouldn't last long restrained, taking orders. Weird how the thought of disappointing him didn't sit well with her. While she continued to value his friendship and the way he and his family had welcomed her into their lives, she'd always considered disappointing others inevitable and part of life. That had certainly been her experience growing up, never able to do enough, be enough to please her parents, or even get their attention.

"The chain." Sucking in a fortifying breath, she took the initiative and reached for the hem of her dress to pull it over her head.

He surprised her when he shook his head and brushed her hands aside. "That's my job, but you do have a say so, if you'd rather start clothed."

Resentment formed a knot in her stomach. She didn't want to stand out as a "newbie," or have him compare her unfavorably with the other, experienced women he'd put on the chain. Or maybe she didn't want a quick end to this attempted affair, like she thought.

Fudge. There was way too much to think about regarding all this.

As if reading her mind, Randy cupped a hand behind her neck, under her hair, and tilted her head back to meet his descending mouth. The kiss took Mickie's mind off all the uncertainties, his commanding pressure and exploring tongue dancing over hers spiking her arousal, her toes curling against the wood floor. Gripping his muscled shoulders to keep from giving in to her weak knees, she moaned into his mouth, arching against his hard strength as his other arm snaked around her hips and held her tight against him, groin to groin.

His mouth-to-mouth possession encircled within his tall, rock-hard body. Mickie quit arguing with herself and embraced the sensation overload. Nothing should feel so good, no one should possess the power to render her incapable of coherent thought, but she couldn't deny or turn down the promise in the way he moved his lips over hers, thrust his rigid cock against her mound, and kept her from falling with his tight hold on her hip.

By the time Randy released her throbbing lips, she wanted nothing more than to strip and feel those large, rough hands on her bare skin. She fought against the intense need consuming her with an attempt at lightheartedness.

"Wow, Sir, you sure know how to show a girl a good time. No wonder you have no trouble getting a woman. Word must have gotten around."

Instead of smiling, he narrowed his eyes, subjecting her to one of those long, disconcerting stares before saying, "I sense my past relationships are an issue with you. Let me assure you, you'll have my undivided attention while we're together. No other woman, or memory of one, will come between us or distract me from your needs."

With a quick shift of his hands, he lifted her dress over her head and tossed it on a chair behind him without turning around. His accuracy would impress her if she weren't shivering under his heated, thorough inspection of her satin covered breasts. His words shouldn't please her so much, something she vowed to get under control later. Much later, Mickie decided as he lifted one arm up and attached a cuff dangling on the end of the chain around her wrist.

"In case no one has instructed yet, the club safe word is red. Saying it will stop whatever we're doing without questions or argument. If you're unsure, say yellow." He skimmed his hand down the underside of her arm, his callouses scraping the sensitive skin, her breath snagging as he cupped her breast. "Nice," he said, flicking his thumb over the nipple. "And fucking responsive."

"And small, don't forget small," she returned, defensive because everyone here seemed to enjoy bigger breasts than her B cups. "What's with all the big boobs anyway?"

Mickie narrowed her eyes as he fought a grin at her disgruntlement. Squeezing the plump mound, he shook his head. "Perfect. I never imagined you would be insecure about your body."

"I'm not," she snapped, yanking on her arm, more annoyed with herself than him. "Can we just get on with this?"

"Nope, and watch your mouth." Reaching behind her, he slapped her butt, the quick sting and burn robbing her breath. "Just a sample if you're not careful. Do you want your other hand tethered or left free?"

She wasn't about to appear wimpy, not with the way he was so comfortable in his role as a Dom. "By all means, give me the full treatment," she answered, raising her arm.

Cuffing her wrist, Randy never took his eyes off her. "I've said it before and likely will again — that attitude of yours will get you in a bind, kid. Remember the time you got pissed because I said you weren't ready to try your hand at breaking a bronco? I think it was Steven who hauled your ass out of the water trough when you went behind our backs."

"But I stayed on far longer than you thought. Admit it," she taunted smugly, the fun memory helping to take her mind off standing there in heels and underwear in a room full of people.

"You always had a way of surprising me," he murmured, his eyes traveling down to her panties, along with his hand. "I like your underwear. It's as silky soft as your skin."

Mickie's heart skipped a beat as he dipped

a finger under the band and caressed the tender flesh left bare from her Brazilian wax. Shawn and Lisa paused as they came by, their sudden presence distracting her as she noticed the dim lighting picked up hints of auburn in the sheriff's dark brown hair. It took every ounce of her determination to keep from squirming in front of the other man, but at least Lisa's friendly smile helped ease her embarrassment.

Randy greeted them with a nod, his fingers gliding over her abdomen in a soft tickle. "It's nice to see you again, Lisa. Other than the second floor, Shawn, the place looks the same. It's been good seeing the familiar faces again."

Shawn nodded. "Make sure you take time to check out the upstairs. We added a new bed I think you'll like in Room 3. Let's get together later tonight to discuss our offer further if you're free then."

"I can be, and again, not necessary but much appreciated."

Shawn surprised Mickie when he leaned forward without releasing Lisa and kissed her cheek. "You're in good hands, but I suspect you know that better than I."

Bemused, she watched them walk off. "This is so different than I expected."

"Good different?" Randy asked.

Returning her gaze to him, she went hot at his intense regard. "I'll let you know."

"You do that."

Determined to put a positive spin on Mickie's first experience, ensuring it was a good one, Randy forced himself to go slow, fighting the urge riding him to take, to stake a claim he couldn't wrap his head around wanting after all this time. He delighted in running his hands over her slender body, her toned muscles and petite breasts a turn-on he never would have suspected he could feel for her. Skimming her sides, he brushed her silk-covered nipples then slipped inside the dainty cups to circle each nub with his thumbs.

Leaning in, he whispered against her mouth, "Edging toward good, if I believe your body and these tight, little nipples. Do you have any idea how fucking arousing your quick responses are?"

"Since this is a first for me, the obvious answer is no," she returned with a breathless catch.

She wasn't shying away from the public exposure, so he unhooked the front bra clasp, keeping his eyes on hers. "Surely not the first time you've had a man's hands on you."

Her derisive reply came with one of her eye

rolls. "Of course not. I meant..."

"I know what you meant. I just enjoy pushing your buttons." Randy cupped her breasts, scraping his nails across her pretty pink nipples and watching them turn to a deeper rose hue. "You like that rougher touch."

"It's...different."

He dug his nails into the tender flesh again. "Is that going to be your answer to everything, it's different?"

Mickie's gray eyes darkened to pewter, a sign of her growing frustration with him. "It's an honest answer. What more do you want?"

Releasing one soft breast, he delivered another harder swat to her ass. "I warned you to watch your tone. You can talk to me without the attitude, at least while we're here. Unless you want to say red already." He issued the challenge on purpose, to goad her into continuing in case she was thinking about stopping because she didn't like that rule.

She narrowed her eyes, clenching her hands into fists. "Finish what you started, Master Randy."

Exactly what I wanted to hear. "If you insist." He bent his head and drew one turgid tip into his mouth, suckling and hollowing his cheeks to pull upward, elongating her nipple into an enticing peak.

She gasped, thrusting her hips forward in a silent plea for more. "You please me very much, Mickie," he said, trailing his mouth up her arched neck.

"Ditto, Sir. Who would have thought?" she murmured with a hint of confusion.

He licked her other nipple then glided his hands downward, over her quivering abdomen to slip inside her panties. "Not me, but unlike you, I'm more than willing to see where this might go."

"I'm standing here tied and naked, aren't I?"

Randy fingered her damp slit, kissing her hard and fast. "Yes, but I can see the reluctance on your face to accept what you're feeling is coming from me, or that we might have a shot at success with changing our relationship."

Jutting her hips into his hand, she closed her eyes on a groan. "Can we just deal with this and discuss anything else later?"

"If that's what you want. Do you want to climax here or in private? Keep in mind, this is the only time I'll let you decide."

Her eyes snapped open, her breath rushing out as she replied, "I swear, if you make me wait, I'll kick you."

"At least you remembered to keep your tone civil when issuing that threat. That's a start."

He thrust two fingers inside her slick pussy, not surprised when her muscles clamped around them, given how wet she was. Rasping her clit as he pulled back, he demanded, "Come for me, Mickie," and plunged deep inside her again.

Throwing her head back, her hair swayed around her back, her arched, slender neck revealing her throbbing pulse as she ground her crotch against his pummeling hand with tiny mewls of pleasure. He pressed his palm against her bare flesh, relishing the damp softness inside and out, and the contrasting difference of her hot, stiff clit.

Inserting his thumb, Randy circled the bundle of nerves, issuing another order. "Now, Mickie."

Mickie exploded in a bright white heat, her body convulsing with pleasure so intense, she grew lightheaded. Forgetting where she was, she rode Randy's hand with unabashed wantonness, eager to reap every ounce of ecstasy possible from his possession. She didn't care who saw, about rules or minding them, only about enjoying a heightened sexual climax she'd never dreamed possible, making every other orgasm she ever experienced pale in comparison.

"Oh God." She moaned, slow awareness seeping

through her fogged senses. Randy never paused in slapping her bare butt in tune with his slower finger thrusts, the steady, light smacks building a heat that matched her fiery response and stunned her by increasing her waning arousal to another feverish pitch. "I can't...*please.*" She was so awash in sensation, she couldn't figure out what she was saying, or begging for.

"Yes, you can," he insisted in a dark voice. "Again, Mickie."

Powerless to resist his and her body's demands, she splintered apart again, the second climax to claim her faculties as intense and mind numbing as the first. Un-*fudging* believable was her only coherent thought as she rode the waves up and then coasted down by slow degrees.

"Are you with me?"

Randy's raspy voice filtered through the euphoric fog clouding her head, his hands cupping her face, bringing Mickie back to full awareness of her surroundings. "I think so."

She avoided glancing around at the people nearby. Their low voices, the snap of leather against bare skin followed by a strident cry, and the soft beat of a soothing song blended together. Her buttocks tingled with lingering warmth, her pussy still pulsated, and she ached all over in the most pleasant way, making it difficult for her to come to terms with how easily she had let go here, in public, with Randy commanding her.

"We need to talk," he stated, releasing her arms, catching her as she sagged against him, and holding her close.

His arms felt good, too good. "Later." Mickie needed some quiet alone time to assimilate what she'd experienced. "I think I want to call it a night." She hoped he wouldn't argue or insist on a soul-baring conversation.

Hooking her bra before loosening his other arm, he said, "All right, but only because I know you can handle what you're feeling well enough on your own for the time being. We'll talk more tomorrow."

Mickie didn't waste time arguing, slipping her dress over her head when he held it up. "Thanks." She sighed, tugging it down, the simple garment offering her armor against the unaccustomed vulnerability seeping in past her lowered defenses.

"Come." Taking her arm, he led her toward the bar. "Take a minute to drink some water and give me time to make sure you're okay to drive."

Annoyance crept past her sluggishness. "I'm not a kid. I can drive home just fine."

"Regardless, you'll wait."

It was much easier obeying him when his hands were on her, but, for expediency, she let his hard insistence go and took the bottled water he handed her. As she drank, he turned to the green-eyed man next to him who looked familiar, but Mickie couldn't remember where she'd seen him before.

"Ben, it's good to see you again," Randy greeted him, shaking his hand.

"I heard you were back, maybe for good this time. I hope that rumor is true. It hasn't been the same without you."

"With my dad's retirement, they need me more. I'm still glad to work with Mickie as our new foreman, though." Reaching for her hand, Randy pulled her to stand in front of him, between his spread knees, facing Ben. "You remember Mickie Taylor, don't you?"

"Sure do." Ben dipped his head, gazing at her with humor. "Park Ranger Wilkins," he reminded her, seeming to read her face with as much accuracy as Randy as she searched her memory for where she knew him. "I helped your dad home one night about five years ago. You were waiting up for him."

No wonder she didn't remember him right away. That was one of those embarrassing incidents involving her parents she just as soon forget. Her dad had run his car off the road coming home from a night visiting the bars in Boise, the loud fight he had with her mother that drove him away resuming the minute he returned. Neither cared about her or Ben's presence. She had cut that visit short and gone back to Colorado the next day.

"Yes, I now recall. Nice to see you again." Between the reminder of that upsetting incident and her head still fuzzy from climaxing while trying to come to terms not only with that release in public but at the hands of Randy, she couldn't think of much else to say.

"You, too. Have either of you met my fiancée?" he asked, holding out his hand to the sun-streaked brunette who joined them.

Randy's mouth twisted into a wry grin. "I thought I heard this rumor. What the hell? I get divorced, and everyone else gets hitched. What's with that?"

"Our good luck and your misfortune," Ben replied with a shrug, running his hand down the woman's arm. "Amie, this is the original owner of Spurs, Master Randy, and Mickie, both natives of Mountain Bend. Amie's from Omaha."

Amie's smile lit up her blue eyes. "Hello," she

replied, leaning against Ben.

"Another transplant. Welcome, Amie. Mickie is ready to call it a night, but I'll be back to hear how you managed to snag this guy."

Thankful for Randy's astuteness, Mickie handed him the empty water bottle and smiled at Amie, returning her hello as he ushered her toward the entry. Her lingering confusion over the night's events and the way her body still hummed with pleasure made it difficult to concentrate on anything else. She needed alone time to gather her thoughts and wrap her head around what this might mean for her long time, close relationship with Randy.

They were both silent until they reached her vehicle and he opened the door. "Maybe I should follow you, make sure you get home safely."

She stiffened and pulled away from him, sliding behind the wheel. "No. I'm fine, Randy. I'll be at the ranch early on Monday." Reaching for the handle, she gritted her teeth when he didn't let go, then held her breath as he bent down.

"Come out tomorrow for lunch. We'll talk."

He kissed her, slow and deep, resurrecting the heat she thought had cooled for the night. "I'll let you know," Mickie answered when he lifted his head. She could see in the overhead light how her evasive answer frustrated him, but that was his problem. She had her own to deal with.

"That'll have to do, for now. Good night."

Mickie drove home wishing the warm fuzzy around her chest would go away. There were enough idiosyncrasies going on with her regarding him to get a handle on. By the time she parked in front of the trailer, mental and physical exhaustion were dragging her down, and the last thing she needed to end the night was a confrontation with her dad. She could only hope the light still showing through the front window meant he had fallen into a drunken sleep in his recliner, not waiting for her to return.

She entered quietly, but it didn't matter. He was not only still awake but still drunk. Lurching to his feet, he swayed and glared at her as she closed the door.

"'Bout fucking time."

Her hackles rose, and she returned his angry glare. "Gee, Dad, I could swear you banned that word years ago. Why are you still up?"

"Don't get sarcastic with me, girl. I burned my hand on that pan, and it's all over the floor. You didn't answer your phone when I called for you to come clean it up before we get cockroaches."

Tired and getting angrier with him by the

second, she tried walking around him to go to her room, but he grabbed her arm and swung her around. Smelling the alcohol on his breath, she took a step back but couldn't pull away from his tight hold.

"Release me," she demanded, furious. "I'm not your maid or here to serve at your beck and call."

Squeezing tighter until she winced from the pain, he snarled, "You'll do as I say, girl, without the sass. I had enough of that from your mother."

"And if you don't want me to walk out of your life like she did, get your *fucking* hand off me."

The slap came so hard and fast it left her reeling, the side of her face exploding with pain. How could she egg him on like that after never forgetting that was his exact reaction the one and only time she heard her mother utter the profanity? She deserved the pain and small cut on her lip bleeding into her mouth for her stupidity, but that didn't mean she would take his abuse without a fight.

Lifting her foot, she kicked him in the crotch, aiming with her heel. He released her arm with a shout of stunned agony and bent over, his ruddy face turning pale. Without a word, she hightailed it out the door to her truck, glad she still held her purse. Mickie drove to the Daniels' ranch without conscious awareness of where she was heading, her throbbing cheek reminding her what an idiot she was. Tears pricked her eyes, but she blinked them away, determined to put this incident behind her just as fast as every other one involving one or both her parents.

Chapter Seven

"Are you sure about this? It's not necessary just because I've returned." Randy's gaze included the three men he sold Spurs to last year. Seated in the office, the faint strains of music and voices filtered through the closed door.

"I am."

"Still a man of few words, I see," he told Dakota.

Clayton smirked. "He talks more when Poppy goads him."

Leaning back in his chair, he eyed his long-time friends with a grin. "All three of you appear happy with your spouses and your decision to settle down." At one time, he'd believed the solution to the dissatisfaction plaguing him was going for the same thing. He was still trying to decide if he was mistaken in what he wanted or in his pick to make that change with. "I missed a lot by staying away from the club whenever I visited." *Like Mickie's recent interest.*

Shawn slid a pen across the desk, prodding him to sign as he said, "Speaking of changing events — you and Mickie?"

"You didn't miss that change, you witnessed it firsthand. Surprised me as much as you." And that was an understatement. He was still working through the ramifications of how much he desired the attitude-riddled, fiercely independent girl whose mature, slim, soft-but-strong body responded to his touch and commands like a wet dream.

"The special ones have a way of doing that." Dakota scrawled his name on the contract and slid it over to Clayton before his black-eyed, direct look dared Randy to deny his observation, which he couldn't do.

"She's always held a special place within my family," he admitted, signing the generous offer and changing the subject. "I haven't checked out your upper level addition yet, but I'm happy to put some cash toward the renovation."

When Clayton and Dakota shook their heads, Shawn replied, "Appreciated but not necessary. The increase in membership has been an unexpected boon."

Randy nodded. "I met Neil Pollono and Nick Rossi."

Clayton was the last to sign off on the document so he could take it to his notary. "They're good fits here. Neil is a ranger with Ben. Nick raises quarter horses and is the best farrier in the state, if you're lucky enough to get him."

"I'll remember that." Getting to his feet, Randy held his hand out to each man. "I'm looking forward to our partnership. I can close tonight for you, to seal the deal."

Shawn stood and shook his hand. "Thanks, but we're already covered. I'll add you to the rotation, though, as well as put you on the list of monitors."

They re-entered the main room, but Randy found himself uninterested in extending the night, even when he caught sight of Kathie bound facing the St. Andrew's Cross, her back and ass arched to accept the flick of Simon's thin cane. Her red-striped buttocks clenched, and he pictured Mickie up there, moaning as he peppered her cheeks with a paddle, an image that would never have entered his head before tonight. How had things changed so fast, so drastically between them?

Left with so many unanswered questions, the least of which where she would be willing to go from here, he made his farewells and called it a night. Suspecting Mickie would make up an excuse to skip lunch with him tomorrow, he contemplated ideas to change her mind on the drive home. Seeing her truck parked in front of the stable surprised him, his first thought something must be wrong. Maybe the calf she had doctored for barbed wire cuts needed additional care. If so, she wouldn't hesitate to come out late at night to attend his injuries. He remembered the time when she was fifteen and spent the night in Black Jack's stall when he suffered with a bout of colic. No amount of talk or threats moved her. She possessed a drive to see things done by her own hand, an admirable trait, and worrisome to those who cared about her.

The lone, bare light bulb lit at the back of the stable cast shadows along the stalls as Randy strode down the center aisle. He paused to stroke behind Black Jack's ears when the stallion stuck his head over the gate.

"Yeah, I know it's late, boy, but where is our girl, *mmm*?"

A sound from the tack room drew him that way, and looking into the room from under the bulb, he could make out Mickie's light hair where she lay on the cot, facing the wall. The heels she wore to the club were on the floor, and he could see the thin dress strap over her shoulder with the light blanket draped across her arm.

A heavy sigh came from her huddled form, and he went over to her. Curious and a touch concerned, he laid a hand on her shoulder. "Mickie, what's going on?"

Her shoulder hunched in an effort to pull away, the move setting off his radar. "I'm fine. Leave me alone."

"Nope, not in this lifetime. Talk to me, baby."

She surprised the hell out of him when she rolled over and socked him in the gut with her balled-up fist.

"What the fuck is wrong with you?" he demanded, rubbing his abdomen.

"Don't ever call me baby again," she snapped, shoving her hair out of her face.

"Hell, Mickie, it's just..." Clamping his mouth shut, he grabbed her chin, tilted her head toward the light, and swore.

"Hey!"

She tried pushing his hand away, but he held firm, every muscle going taut with his anger at seeing her swollen lip. "Who did this?"

Mickie closed her eyes, and he noticed the strain etched on her face. "Let it go. It's no big deal, leave me alone."

"Again, not now, not ever."

She gave him an eye roll then glared. "Look..."

Exasperated with her stubbornness, he scooped her up and tossed her over his shoulder. "What...are you doing, you moron?" she stuttered with a half laugh.

"Taking you to my house. You're not sleeping out here like the hired hands. And, come morning, you will talk to me." But he already knew her father was responsible for her bruised, cut mouth.

"I *am* a hired hand," she huffed.

He kept quiet, lowering her onto the passenger seat of his truck, trying to figure out exactly what she was to him now. He breathed a sigh of relief when she stayed put after he slammed the door and stalked around to the driver's side. Getting behind the wheel, he started the engine, his fury still simmering on a low boil. It took supreme effort to delay a confrontation with her old man, but for her sake, that satisfaction would wait until tomorrow.

As he pulled in front of his house, he caught her rubbing her knuckles and grinned. "Hurt your hand?"

"It was like hitting a board," she muttered. "I'll remember that next time."

"Or you could try talking first," he suggested,

opening the door.

Mickie shrugged and let herself out. "Don't lump me in with all your girlfriends, and we won't have a problem."

Ah, so that's it. "Jealous, Mickie?" he taunted, taking her arm and leading her inside.

She snorted. "Not hardly."

"Good, you have no need to be, and I doubt I've been with near as many women as you believe." Mickie had a way of throwing up obstacles when she was insecure, he just wished she would open her mind to exploring a change between them. "Come on. I'm as tired as you." He started down the hall toward his room, but she held back.

"Your guest rooms are that way." She pointed behind her, her face set in a stubborn scowl.

"You're not a guest, and don't argue. I'm not in the mood."

Randy didn't have to turn around to know she rolled her eyes again, too relieved when she accepted one of his T-shirts to sleep in and slid into his bed without another word to question her easy capitulation until she spoke again.

"Don't read anything into this," she mumbled, snuggling under the covers with a sigh. "I'm just too tired to keep sparring with you tonight."

Randy saw what his anger had blinded him to – the shadows of sadness in her eyes before she closed them. First thing in the morning, he would make sure Ed Taylor never put that look on her face again.

Mickie listened to Randy moving about, clicking off lights before undressing. She was still annoyed with his high-handedness, but his shirt carried his scent, the soft cotton enveloping her a comfortable wrap against the lingering cold from her father's actions. It shouldn't bother her so much after all these years, but there was no accounting for her constant hopes either he or her mother would change.

To take her mind off the heartache of what she couldn't control, she pictured Randy naked, his tall body rippling with muscles honed by hard, physical labor. She wondered if his cock was a big as the rest of him then tried to curb that train of thought despite the damp spasm gripping her pussy. Succumbing to the growing need for his full possession while still coming to terms with the scene at the club that led to that off-the-charts climax and vulnerable from her dad's actions wouldn't be wise. It would only lead to more questions about their relationship and more risk of additional hurt when the sex wasn't enough for either of them.

Wise or not, her body didn't care when the bed dipped and he pulled her back against his front, spooning her from behind, his body heat enough to dispel the remaining chill from her father's betrayal. Never one to shy away from the obvious, she admitted she wouldn't get the sleep she craved to put this night behind her without his help or giving in to the lust clamoring for relief in a way only Randy had inspired.

Turning in his arms, she couldn't make out his features with the only light coming from the white glow of the moon through the window, but the shape of his broad shoulders and wide chest were easy to find in the dark using her hands.

"This is just sex," she whispered against his mouth, running her palms from his shoulders down his arms while rubbing her mound against his erection. "Agreed?"

Randy rolled her onto her back, his big body pressing her down onto the mattress as he loomed above her. "Sex my way, agreed?" He punctuated that inquiry with a slow glide of his rigid cock over her panty-covered pussy lips.

Mickie's breath stalled as she shook with

anticipation so acute, she would agree to anything. Forgetting he didn't admit this was just sex, she strained to arch her hips upward but failed, his lower body keeping her pinned in place. Her heart stuttered, that loss of control sending a wave of uncertainty through her. At the club, only her arms were restrained, leaving her lower body free, a boon she just realized.

"Randy." Mickie gritted her teeth against the quiver in her voice. Annoyed, she started to say, "Look—" but he cut her off by cradling her face in his hands and brushing a light kiss over her puffy lip.

"Trust is a hard thing to earn, easy to lose, and never to be taken lightly. I would think, after all these years, I've earned yours, and I sure as hell would never risk losing it at this point."

There in the dark, the deep rumble of his familiar voice washed away her insecurities. She had trusted him at the age of ten, and conceded she could do no less now, especially since the rest of her was on board with his sexual control. "Okay, fine, just, don't make me wait. I need this."

"Funny, I was thinking the same thing," he murmured, levering himself up enough to whisk the shirt off, followed by yanking her panties down. Coming back over her naked body, he sighed. "Much better."

Much, she thought, relishing the skin-to-skin contact. His hair-roughened thighs spread hers, and she didn't hesitate to wrap her legs around his lean hips, enjoying the nipple tickles from his crisp chest hair.

"Now," she insisted, desperate to lose herself in pleasure again, to the exclusion of everything else, including what changes tomorrow would bring.

"My way, remember? And I want to enjoy you. You're so soft." He took his hand down her side and slid under her butt to squeeze one cheek. Dipping his head, his whiskers lightly scratched her breast as he licked the puckered tip. "These little jewels are so fucking hard."

Mickie strained against him, rubbing her labia along his cock, wishing he didn't have to suit up before entering her. She'd love to feel those bare ridges rasping her insides. "And you're hard everywhere." She worked a hand behind then under him, grazing his taut buttocks on her way to roll his balls in her palm then grip his cock. "Really hard." Tightening her fingers around his girth, she nipped his lower lip.

"You're pushing me, Mickie." Randy shuddered as she stroked his shaft then rubbed the smooth crown between her folds. "Enough," he growled on a harsh breath, pulling her hand off his flesh. "You'll pay for ignoring my wishes but not tonight."

The threat didn't faze her, not when he was groping for a condom from the side table then struggling to don it with her legs still clutching his lower back. She could loosen them and give him more room but didn't want to risk losing her tenuous grip on the man she could have sworn she'd stopped craving this way years ago.

"Yes, *please*," she pled as he nudged his latex-covered cock head inside her.

Randy groaned, pushing deeper. "Shit, you're tight." Returning to grasp her buttock, he dug his fingers into her cheek and held tight. "Brace yourself," he warned.

Mickie latched onto his upper arms as he surged inside her pussy, the heat lashing her nerve endings with his plunging stroke consuming her with lust. With just one hand holding her pelvis still for his pummeling rampage, he left her no choice but to lie under him and take his rough possession. Instead of pissing her off, or detracting from her spiraling arousal, her vaginal walls clamped around his clit-rasping cock. Tight as a vise, her inner muscles gripped his steely flesh with a desperate need that was new to her. He ground his hips against hers, eliciting the smaller contractions that prepared her for a full release, drawing a low moan from her throat.

She gave up trying to regain the sanity his fierce thrusts had stolen. He grunted above her, ramming between her legs, shocking her when he breached her anus with one finger. Jabbing those untouched nerve endings in tune with his hammering cock sent her over the edge, frenzied waves of fiery pleasure undulating through her entire body and rippling up and down her fiercely clutching pussy.

Randy put his mouth to her ear, his labored, raspy voice penetrating the euphoric haze as he continued to grind into her. "That's my girl, Mickie, give me everything."

Left with no choice, she embraced the oblivion of another shattering climax then the exhaustion that claimed her before she came fully back to her senses.

****

Randy didn't like when women came on to him or when one made demands of him, and in the fifteen years since his interest in sexual domination had grabbed hold, he had rejected any woman who did so. Until last night. When Mickie turned to him, soft and warm, her voice carrying a note of desperation in the dark he'd never heard from her before, he'd been unable to turn her away. The fact he wanted her more than his next breath also played a role in giving in when she initiated sex.

In all the years he'd known her, she never showed any outward signs of emotional distress over her parents' dysfunctional relationship and indifference. He'd seen her angry, frustrated, and blasé following one of their blowouts, but never upset. Of course, neither of them had struck her before, either. At least, not that he was aware. If she kept something like that from him, they would have more to discuss than this change in their relationship when he got back.

The rising sun hadn't made it past a yellow/ orange sliver peeking over the mountains when he slid out of bed without waking Mickie. After carrying his clothes into the guest bathroom to shower and dress, he brewed a pot of coffee, poured some in an insulated, covered cup, and left while she still slept. He would deal with her attitude when he returned from a long overdue talk with her old man.

Once he arrived, Randy wasted no time storming up to the trailer door and pounding before letting himself inside. Empty beer bottles and trash were strewn around the small living room, and from the doorway, he could see a pan lying upside down on the kitchen floor and ants crawling around the spilled contents. Disgusted, he turned toward the hall when he heard Ed mumbling and stumbling around.

Rubbing his eyes, he muttered, "Who? Daniels. What do you want?"

"I want to plant my fist in your face, so if you wish to avoid that painful retribution, sit your ass down and pay close attention to me."

Ed glared at him. "Who the hell do you think you are, coming in here uninvited and making demands? Do you know what time it is?"

Randy snatched Ed's arm, almost reeling from the man's alcohol-and-sweat odor, and shoved him into the worn recliner. Leaning over, he snarled, "I *know* I'm the only one who's stood up for your daughter. Lay a hand on her again and I'll tear you apart. Are we clear?"

Ed paled, and there was no denying the shocked surprise on his face. "What are you talking about?" he asked hoarsely. "I've never raised my hand to that girl."

"You did last night, hard enough to give her a

cut, bruised mouth and puffy cheek."

Ed shook his head in denial. "I don't remember, I swear...it's been so hard with Stacy leaving..."

Randy remained unmoved by the older man's obvious distress. "Don't give me that bullshit. You two spent thirty years making each other and your daughter miserable. Here's what you're going to swear to. Start cleaning up around here, take care of yourself, go back to the mill and ask for a desk job. And don't fucking piss me off again."

With that, he left Ed sitting there while he collected Mickie's clothes from her old room. Tossing whatever he could find she had unpacked back into the two suitcases on the floor, he closed them up and carried them out.

Unable to stomach another moment in Ed's presence or inside the trailer's foul condition, he went straight for the door. Reaching for the handle, he paused as Ed asked in a trembling voice, "What are you doing with her things?"

He glanced around, taking the time to deliver one parting piece of advice. "Making sure Mickie doesn't have a reason to come back here until you straighten up. You've already driven away your wife. If I were you, I would make whatever changes necessary to keep my daughter from following in her footsteps."

He slammed out and inhaled a much-needed breath of fresh air. He'd always admired Mickie's loyalty to parents who didn't deserve it, but now it both baffled and enraged him, how much she'd given them over the years without receiving an ounce of love or support in return. Taking his time driving home, he worked to get himself under control and set aside his disgust with Ed.

Randy stopped at the barn seeing Lance exit and wave to him. Leaning his arm on the open window sill, he asked, "What's up, Lance?"

"I noticed Mickie's truck but couldn't find her. Firestorm is limping again, and I checked his hoof. He's got another abscess and needs antibiotics if she has some in the cabinet. Do you know where she is?"

He nodded, refusing to sidestep the change in their relationship. "Up at my house. She showed up late after an argument with her dad." The hands were aware of the nearby private club and his former ownership of Spurs, but it wasn't his place to reveal Mickie's recent involvement.

"That's too bad. I've never met the man but heard about her mother taking off." When Randy nudged his hat up and lifted a brow, Lance shrugged off admitting he listening to rumors. "Hey, it's a small town. You can't avoid gossip."

"Yeah, you've got that right. Still, don't spread any when you see her bruised mouth," he warned.

Lance's jaw went rock hard, his eyes flat as he gave him a curt nod. "No way, Boss. Is she okay?"

"Yes. She's too stubborn not to be. I'll tell her about Firestorm. I'm sure there are some antibiotics in the cabinet." The black-and-white Pinto was an excellent cutter horse and needed out on the range, so the sooner they could get his hoof healed, the better for the horse and their workload.

"Thanks. Catch you later."

Bracing himself for the confrontation waiting for him up at his house, he replied, "Later, then," and continued that way.

Mickie rounded on Randy the second he entered his house carrying her bags. "Where have you been? You left me here knowing I wasn't about to trek down to my truck in heels." Her stormy gaze landed on her suitcases. "What did you do?" she whispered, her tone a furious whiplash.

Dropping the bags, he fisted his hands on his hips. "I informed your deadbeat, abusive father you wouldn't return until he could keep his hands off you. If you have a problem with that, tough. Given the change in our relationship, it makes sense for you to stay here."

She narrowed her eyes and mimicked his stance by placing her balled hands on her hips. He tried not to get distracted by the sudden recall of her bare legs gripping his waist and her feet digging into his lower back as he pounded into her tight, slick heat. God, he'd loved fucking her, hearing her little mewls of pleasure, her tight convulsions squeezing his sperm out of his balls to spew from his cock head.

"Just what change are you referring to, Randy? Surely you don't expect me to kowtow to your whims twenty-four seven just because we slept together?"

"Newsflash, Mickie," he said, stalking forward until he stood toe to toe with her. Cupping her chin, he held her face up, settling his other hand on her right buttock. "We weren't sleeping the whole night, and the sex was at your insistence. Are you brave enough to see through what you started, or not?"

She tried jerking away, but Randy tightened both hands and was rewarded with one of her insolent eye rolls. "For God's sake, it was sex, just sex, nothing more, and nothing you haven't indulged in countless times before with countless women."

"Is that what you think?" he drawled.

With every other woman before her, including Melanie at first, she was correct. He cared about seeing to their needs, but beyond that goal, those past relationships hadn't extended beyond the physical. For a while, way too long, he'd believed he and Melanie shared a special connection, but by the time he finally pulled his head out of his ass and gotten over her betrayal, he realized she'd bruised his ego more than his heart. A bitter pill to swallow, for sure, but behind him now.

"Yes, it is. But you're right, I started it, and, if you want an affair, fine, but remember, I'm not submissive like your ex."

"That remains to be seen. Time will tell, won't it? In the meantime, when we're at the club or anywhere else you believe we're indulging in just sex, it's Master Randy." He kissed her mulish mouth. "And you could sound and look happier about it."

Relief erased her disgruntled expression as he dropped his hands and stepped back. "I know it's your day off, but Lance says Firestorm has come up lame again. Can you check him out before taking off on Black Jack?"

She cocked her head. "How did you know I planned to ride this afternoon?"

"Please, Mickie. Give me some credit for the years you've spent as part of my family. I have paperwork to catch up on. Feel free to put your clothes in my closet. I'll drive you down to the stable when you're ready."

Chapter Eight

More than sex? Mickie scoffed at the idea. *No way, I won't let it.* With Randy's history of preferring submissive, malleable women, it would be idiocy to agree with him. He couldn't even stay married to one. Okay, that wasn't fair, she conceded. Melanie had cheated on him, and from what Caroline had told her, he wasted no time filing for divorce and booting her out when he learned of her infidelity.

Mickie reached for the door handle, looking at Randy. Like her, he loved the outdoors, and it showed in his tanned, rugged profile, his face more mature yet the same as when she first set eyes on him. She was always more comfortable with the familiar, and other than her parents, she'd thought no one in her life, past or present, was as well-known to her as this man. Yet, for the life of her, she couldn't figure out what he wanted from her now, or how to give it to him without setting herself up to get hurt again.

"You're thinking too hard, Mickie." Randy leaned over and brushed that sexy mouth over her lips.

The gentle touch to her bruised mouth reminded her of his earlier high-handedness, and she used that topic to divert his attention from her effort to accept this change he wanted. "I can handle my dad, and I'm not afraid of him."

"No, you never were, of him or anything else that I'm aware of. But make him take responsibility for his actions, all of them. If you continue to cater to him, he'll continue to take advantage of your misplaced familial loyalty."

"You wouldn't do the same for Ron and Caroline?"

"I most definitely would, the difference being their exemplary parenting and unconditional love the past thirty-eight years opposed to your folks' self-centered neglect and now abuse of you." He pinched her chin. "Erase that pigheaded expression. You don't have to like it, but you know I'm right. Go. I have to get to the tedious paperwork waiting for me."

She opened the door and hopped down then slammed it shut without another word. He *was* right, and she *didn't* like it but agreed it would be best if she gave her parent time to cool down and think about his actions. Since Randy insisted on this change between them, at least she could look forward to more of those mind-numbing orgasms to distract her from worrying.

Mickie made her way to Firestorm's stall and checked the horse's hoof. "Yep, you've managed to get yourself infected again." She dropped his leg and patted his shoulder. "Be right back."

"Do they ever answer you?" Lance asked, holding the stall gate open.

"Sure, with a nudge or head brush against me." Glancing in the next stall at the calf, she said, "This one can rejoin the herd today. I'll take him if you can't."

"I planned to ride up to that pasture shortly, when I finish in the barn. Go ahead and take Black Jack out when you're done with Firestorm. I'll get this guy back to his momma."

She nodded. "Okay. I'll probably see you there. Black Jack likes to splash in the lake."

After gathering supplies from the medicine cabinet, she tended to Firestorm's abscess, wrapping the hoof in a poultice and administering a dose of antibiotics and painkiller. She found Black Jack saddled and ready for her at the corral and waved to

Lance in appreciation as he entered the massive barn that stored hay, feed, and farming equipment. Two other even larger barns provided winter housing for cattle during the harshest conditions.

Before Randy, his parents, or the hands would let her take on too many chores those first few years, she'd spent hours following them around in those buildings, making a pest of herself and not caring. Lucky for her, none of them seemed to mind her endless questions and constant griping over the way they coddled her, a protectiveness she wasn't used to from anyone. There were few perks to being raised by two people who were more focused on their bitter disagreements with each other than on their only child, and the freedom to run around without supervision, come and go as she pleased, was one of them.

Swinging up onto Black Jack, Mickie's mood lightened as she recalled how many times she'd butted heads with Randy when he tried to keep tabs on her. Leaning forward, she rubbed a hand down the stallion's sleek neck. "He better not try pulling that crap on me again just because we're sleeping together, right, boy?"

Black Jack tossed his head, as if he understood and agreed. Mickie chuckled and steered him toward the wide-open terrain beckoning to them. "Yeah, you always have my back, don't you? Come on, big guy. Let's ride."

They took off at a fast clip, Mickie never tiring of the wind beating at her face, the ground whizzing by, or the woods blurring in her peripheral vision. She basked in her steed's powerful muscles bunching under her as she gripped his sides with her legs and leaned low over his outstretched neck and head. At the age of twenty, he continued to amaze and please her with his stamina and tireless, eager energy.

By the time they reached the lake, they were both winded, the grazing herd paying them no mind as she rode him through the shallow edge. When he paused to drink, she pulled her water bottle from the saddlebag and swallowed the entire contents, reminded of when Randy had insisted on her rehydrating last night at the club before he would escort her out. Out here, far from him and the sex-charged venue where she couldn't resist him or what he offered, she could admit she liked that coddling. His touch, and the climax he'd driven her to, had left her confused and vulnerable, but he hadn't taken advantage of her befuddled state to push her into accepting a change in their relationship. No, that acceptance had come at her insistence in the dark of night.

"There's nothing to do but see it through, right, boy? I mean, we've already crossed the line, may as well go the distance then move on, curiosity satisfied, no regrets." At least, she hoped it would end that way.

Mickie opted to ride back taking one of the wooded trails, getting them both out from under the midafternoon sun. The fresh, clean scent of pine assailed her senses as she and Black Jack wound their way along the wide forest path, the tree-dense area providing a marked edge between the Daniels' property and a county back road. Halfway back, she heard an equine's distinctive stressful whinny followed by the loud, resonating clank of its iron-shod hooves striking what was likely a horse trailer.

Curious, she nudged Black Jack toward the commotion, following the angry male cursing coming from the same direction. They emerged onto the dirt road, and she lifted a hand to shield her eyes against the sun's glare to get a better look at the truck and attached horse trailer up ahead. One man sat crouched by a flat tire, waiting for the second man to bring him a jack, the horse they were hauling clearly unhappy being confined in the cramped space.

Riding forward, she pulled up a few feet away,

halting as soon as both men whipped their heads around, appearing none too happy to see her. "I can give your horse a break from the trailer while you're fixing the flat, if you'd like. It's not good for them to get so agitated." She couldn't tell if the animal was angry, scared, or something in between, only that he needed a reprieve from the close confines.

The baseball-cap-wearing man at the flat peered up at the other guy, who smoothed out the frown he gave her intrusion and offered a smile. "Thanks, ma'am, but he's okay for a few more minutes." He glanced around at the open field behind him. "Is your place nearby?"

She wondered what difference that made then shrugged off her suspicion. From what she could see through the ventilation side slats on the trailer, the white or gray-coated horse was too big to be transported in such a small trailer. No wonder he was so upset. Still, her hands were tied if the owners refused her help.

"I'm not far. Are you sure I can't help? I'm a veterinary assistant and know horses. He could use a respite from the tight enclosure." She tried and failed to keep a note of censure from creeping into her voice. Both men would catch the eye of any red-blooded female, and looked enough alike with their light-brown hair and resembling features to guess they were brothers or cousins, which didn't explain the creepy vibes and skittering nerves she was experiencing.

The same man transferred the replacement tire to his friend, inching his right hand behind him as he took a step toward her. "We're good, and don't have too much farther. I'll give him his favorite treat, and he'll settle down. Why don't you…"

"Mickie!"

Hearing Randy's voice echoing through the trees helped Mickie relax. She attributed her tiredness from the late night's physical activity as the reason for her odd distrust of the two men.

"Looks like I'd better get going. Please don't leave your horse much longer inside that small trailer." Lifting a hand in farewell, she turned Black Jack toward the trail.

"You know what to do, right?" Chuck glared at his brother.

"Yeah, I do. You just concentrate on getting us going again and out of here before anyone else happens by." Fisting his hand, Dex delivered a strong punch to the trailer. "Fucking animal. You'd better bring a good price, or you're dog meat."

"There you are," Randy greeted her as she emerged from the woods.

Mickie sighed. "Please tell me you're not keeping tabs on me."

She couldn't deny the warm rush of pleasure at seeing him, her mind shifting from the poor agitated horse to the memory of those broad shoulders straining his worn, blue-denim work shirt looming over her in the dark. These spontaneous hot flashes of lust were nice perks to indulging in an affair if she could get him to agree that's all this was.

"I learned long ago trying to keep track of your whereabouts was a waste of time." His gaze turned sharp. "Everything okay? You look put out, and not just with me."

He always could read her well, something that had taken her a long time to adjust to and accept. "I came across a couple of guys hauling their horse in a trailer too small for the poor animal's comfort. Their indifference to his suffering pissed me off, but they insisted they didn't have far to go. What's up? I didn't think you planned to ride today."

"I didn't until I thought about dinner. It's getting late and I want to take you out to eat in Boise. I wasn't about to chance starving while waiting for you to return."

The offer surprised her, and she went with the first response that popped up and blurted, "Why?" She almost grinned when she recognized the sigh he released. She'd heard that same exasperated response hundreds of times, and it bothered her as much as any of those other times – not.

Randy ran a hand behind his neck, another sign her reply wasn't what he was used to hearing from women in response to an invitation out. "Because I want to spend time with you, although, for the life of me, I can't figure out why at this moment."

Mickie pulled alongside him as he kicked Cheyenne into a walk, amused at the tight set of his lips. "Surf and turf?" He knew how much she loved steak paired with any seafood, especially her favorite, salmon.

He gave her a curt nod. "The Roadhouse Inn. Salmon's the special tonight."

"I'm in."

He swiveled to face her, and she couldn't read his expression with his Stetson tilted so low it hid his eyes. "There's more to an affair with me than sex, Mickie. Best you accept that, too, and the sooner the better. Let's ride."

Bemused, excited, and yep, a touch annoyed,

she watched him take off without looking back. By the time she shook off all three responses to that comment given in his strict Dom's voice, he was way ahead of her, and she didn't care. She needed the space and extra time to do what he said, get her mind on board with how fast everything was changing between them without a clue as to why and to what end. She was the complete opposite of the type of women he had always preferred, and she couldn't believe he'd changed his mind after all these years of indulging in Dom/sub relationships, both at the club and at home, as his marriage attested.

Time would tell, Mickie supposed. At least she was mature enough to shield her heart from getting hurt this time around.

Even after everything her parents had put her through, Mickie still possessed a soft heart, just one of the traits Randy had always admired about her. Her displeasure with the horse's temporary confinement still lingered on her face when she slipped into his bathroom to freshen up and change clothes. Odds were the steed would be fine, otherwise she would never have ridden away without enlisting help for the equine.

Once when he'd picked her up, she had insisted

he stop by one of their neighbors in the trailer park and put the fear of God in a woman for constantly breeding her small poodle in deplorable conditions. When she threatened to dognap the bitch and her new litter, he offered the woman more money for the dogs than she would make on several more litters. That was one of those rare times Mickie let her guard down long enough to throw her arms around him, exhibiting her profound gratitude instead of just verbalizing her appreciation. Luckily, he had found them all good homes.

Randy waited for her in the living room, giving her some privacy when what he wanted to do the minute they returned was get her naked and drive into her slick tight heat again. Instead of easing after last night, his craving for her continued to maintain a desperate clutch on his balls. He wondered how long it would take to come to terms with wanting the kid he'd regarded as family since the first summer she practically lived at the ranch. The second he saw her last night for the first time wearing a dress and heels, her hair hanging down to her waist instead of braided, he'd seen beyond the woman he was proud of, his mind and body both laying claim to her with one word – *mine*.

Randy was coming to terms with this change

much faster and easier than Mickie, but that was all right. Being a good Dom required patience, more so when dealing with someone so reluctant to change, and admitting to the needs his control exposed. It would be pointless for him to mention again his suspicion she might harbor a small sexual submissive streak. It would be more fun to prove it to her, starting tonight, after dinner.

He turned from the large window offering an expansive view of colorful summer wildflowers stretching as far as the eye could see when he heard her coming down the hall. She'd surprised him by trading blue denim jeans for a white denim skirt and her tee for a rose-colored, sleeveless blouse, her sneakers for sandals. She must not realize how the sight of her bare legs affected him.

"What?" she asked, her silver gaze turning wary.

Stalking toward her, he gave her a rueful grin. "I'm thinking how cool and composed you look when I'm itching to push that skirt up and bend you over the sofa." Cupping her chin, he kissed her, hard and deep, resting his other hand over her chest, the rapid beat of her heart against his palm proof she wasn't as unaffected by him as she was trying to portray.

"I thought you were hungry," she said as soon

as he released her and stepped back.

"Oh, sweetheart, I am."

She narrowed her eyes, setting her mouth in a familiar, mulish line.

"Don't get all pissy. I didn't call you baby."

"Same thing. It's one of your generic, meaningless endearments. News flash – I agreed to continue this, so you don't need to soften me up."

Snatching her hand, he tugged her toward the door. "If *this*, as you call it, is nothing more than an affair, why do you care what I call you?"

"I don't, I just...*fudge*. Shut up, Randy."

He opened the truck door and gripped her waist to hoist her onto the seat.

Her hands went to his shoulders and held tight, her nails digging into his skin, her face close to his.

"Lighten up, Mickie. This is supposed to be fun."

Randy whistled as he strolled around to the driver's side and got behind the wheel. Starting the engine, he changed the conversation around on her. "It's been a while, but why don't you tell me the real reason you canceled our ride the last time you were in town. As I recall, you were the one spouting the generic excuse of being too busy to get away."

Mickie released one of her annoyed huffs then

flashed him a sardonic look. "Dredging up the past isn't fun. Why don't you ask your ex?"

"What's Melanie..." He suddenly remembered Melanie going back inside the restaurant after he'd spoken with Mickie. It wasn't the first time someone mentioned his ex-wife had stuck her nose where it didn't belong. "Fuck. What did she say?"

Her lips quirked. "That isn't a nice word."

"No, it's not. What did she say?"

Rolling her eyes, she shook her head. "It was no big deal. Your wife didn't want me around. I can't blame her."

"I can. You shouldn't have listened to her, in fact, it's not like you to back down." Pulling onto the main road toward Boise, he accelerated, wishing he had wised up about his marriage and his feelings a lot sooner.

Without looking at him, Mickie replied, "It wasn't worth an argument or causing a rift between you two. By then, my life was in Colorado where I spent most of my time, so it didn't matter."

Reading her clearly, he reached over and pinned her hand under his. He hated that Melanie might have caused Mickie even one second of grief or uncertainty about herself or her place on the ranch.

"If you tell me you believed I or anyone else

didn't want you coming around anymore, I'll pull over and spank your delectable ass until I'm sure you'll never make that mistake again."

Instead of delivering an indignant, scathing rejoinder, she burst out laughing. "You...you know... *Master* Randy," she gasped, "dating you could be fun. Spank me if I was dumb enough to let her hurt my feelings." She giggled again, shaking her head with another eye roll.

Randy reached the restaurant and parked, keeping her hand trapped in her lap with his as he said, "You're tempting me, Mickie." *In more ways than one.* Even though he'd known going into this she was a far cry from the meeker, submissive women he was usually drawn to, he found it more difficult than he had guessed to set aside his expectations of compliance for Mickie. "I'm not sure I care for you laughing at my concern for your feelings." Not to mention he suspected her humor was an attempt to cover emotions she wasn't comfortable sharing. She was always careful to keep from revealing any vulnerability, or from leaving herself open for hurt.

Sobering, she regarded him with a thoughtful look before saying, "Sorry, but you should know by now it's not easy to hurt my feelings, and certainly not by one of your exes. There are way too many to waste time over such a frivolous worry."

"You know, kid," he replied, releasing her hand. "We're going to have to discuss this thing you have for bringing up those who came before you." Judging by her frown, she didn't care for him pointing that out.

Opening her door, she hopped down then turned around. "No, we aren't. Come on. I'm hungry."

Yeah, he was going to have to work on keeping himself in check if he wanted to see how far he could take this relationship. The escalating depth of his need for her threatened his usual patience. Mickie grabbed his hand and pulled, tossing him a cheeky grin that caused a funny clutch in his chest, the twitch of her ass hitting him much lower, stirring his cock.

"You can't tempt me with surf and turf then lollygag."

They entered the restaurant, and he leaned down to whisper in her ear. "If only you would show as much enthusiasm for pleasing me as you do for food."

She snorted. "How about you please me first," she whispered back.

"Okay." The glance of suspicion she tossed him

drew his grin. She was right to be wary of his quick agreement.

"Table for two?" the hostess asked, picking up two menus.

"Yes, in a quiet corner, please." The dim interior would benefit his plans, as well as the secluded booth in the rear she led them to. Fewer than half the tables were occupied, which also worked in his favor.

With his back to the hostess, Randy placed a hand on Mickie's butt as she bent to slide into the booth, the small clench of her buttocks enough of a reaction to suit him. Following her, he laid a hand on her thigh under the table as he reached for the menus the hostess held out.

"Your waitress will be right with you. Enjoy your meal."

"Thank you." He turned to Mickie, tightening his hand when she tried putting a little space between them. "Problem?"

"No, not at all." She snapped the menu open, hiding behind it

For someone who was determined to keep him from controlling her, she was so easy to arouse. Damn, he liked that about her.

"Good. I'm going for the steak and shrimp." He

coasted up her smooth thigh, sliding under the skirt edge then moving his thumb in slow circles around the inside of her leg. From the minute shudder that went through her, the light caress was effective.

"We're in public, Randy," she muttered under her breath, tightening her legs.

The waitress was approaching, but the tablecloth kept their legs and his hand hidden. "I know. Steak and salmon for you?"

"Of course," she answered, trying and failing to appear unaffected. Mickie reached for a roll as he gave the girl their orders then she added, "Could I have a bourbon and Coke please?"

"Sure thing. You, sir?"

After ordering a beer and handing the young girl the menus, Randy waited until she walked away before reaching in front of Mickie for a roll, letting his arm brush across her nipples. She sucked in a deep breath at their instant pucker, but before he could say anything as he leaned back, she spoke first.

"If you ask me if I have a problem, I'll pop you. Knock it off."

"Okay, for now, but only because I want you to enjoy your meal." Removing his hand from her leg, he lifted his arm to rest it behind her on top of the booth seat. "Tell me more about your life in

Colorado."

They fell back into their easy banter, Mickie eating two rolls and reaching for a third by the time their orders arrived. It was always a joy watching her eat, as much as eyeing her nonstop energy as she worked off the calories with constant physical activity. He could never imagine her at a desk job.

They were halfway back to the ranch, Mickie appearing content and relaxed from dinner and two drinks with her head leaning against the seat, humming softly. Her mellow mood allowed for her guard to slip and offered the perfect opportunity for him to give her a taste of his domination outside of the club.

"Unbutton your top, Mickie."

Her eyes flew open, and even in the dark cab, he could detect the hard point of her nipples against the thin material.

"Why?"

She tried for a strong note, but he caught the quiver in her voice. "Because it's what I want," he returned.

"Anyone passing by us might see if their headlights are high enough." She glanced out the windshield at the oncoming vehicle approaching from the opposite direction.

"Odds are it won't be anyone you know, so do you care? Don't lie," he warned.

"Fine."

That time, he couldn't tell anything from her tone, but it didn't matter since she obeyed then surprised him when she took it a step further and flicked open her bra. When she cupped her small breasts and teased her nipples with her thumbs, Randy suspected she was trying to exert some control, which meant his commands were threatening her independence. He would let her play for a while then remind her who was boss when it came to this part of their relationship.

Chapter Nine

Mickie shocked herself with her brazen behavior, but it was either try to distract Randy from exerting his usual dominance or succumb to a need that was more than sexual that his rough-voiced instructions continued to pull from her. She wasn't ready to admit she liked the way he took over, leaving her free to not only indulge in the myriad of sensations she'd never felt with other men, but to drop her guard on her emotions for a short period.

Warm tingles spread across her nipples as she thumbed the tender nubs. She'd always found touching herself a pleasurable alternative when the mood struck for intimacy, and she wasn't in a relationship. But with Randy sitting so close, knowing he kept glancing over at her yet unable to read his expression in the dark, every cell in her body inflamed with a heightened awareness that was new to her. Masturbation had always been a private indulgence, and she'd never imagined the titillating effect of having an audience. But this was Randy, the person she trusted most, above all others, the only one she'd let herself care for on a deeper level than friendship.

Determined to prevent those deeper feelings from getting trampled on again, she tweaked and rolled her nipples in a way she'd always enjoyed, reminding herself of all the women who had come before her and those likely to follow.

"I didn't give you permission to touch yourself, Mickie." Without warning, Randy reached over, delved under her skirt, and ran a finger between her legs, slipping under the edge of her panties. She sucked in a breath as he swiped up her slit then brought his finger to his mouth and licked. "*Mmm.* Considering this, I'll allow you to continue."

Allow? That comment got her back up, but before she let loose with a scathing retort, he drawled, "I wouldn't, if I were you. You agreed any time we were engaged in a sexual scenario, you would abide by my rules, and you're the one who has already overstepped."

"You started it." Okay, that sounded petulant, but damn it, her buttocks clenched, the dark edge to his tone that hinted at retribution sending a familiar wave of heat sweeping through her.

"Which is my prerogative, not yours. Dampen a finger in your pussy then wipe it off on your nipples, and keep doing that until both are well-coated," he instructed, this time without taking his eyes off the road.

Mickie jerked, her sheath spasming in response. "Why?" she asked automatically, and damn if her voice didn't quaver again.

"Mickie," he growled, his tone warning enough without further words.

She'd never considered herself a prude but was grateful for the dark cab when her face went hot. His decadent commands were getting to her on a level she didn't quite understand yet found herself willing to explore, just for him, just with him. It didn't help when the approaching SUV passed by, their headlights high enough to illuminate the front seat for one split second. From the quick horn blast, that was apparently long enough to catch a glimpse of her breasts. Her nipples pulsed in reciprocation, the traitorous little bitches.

Since Mickie couldn't decide whether the compulsion to please Randy or to push his control buttons was strongest, she decided obeying that order would work either way. While leaving her left hand holding her breast, she slid her right under her panties, scooting her hips forward on the seat so she could delve deeper inside her pussy and swirl her finger. It was impossible not to rub her clit in the process, setting off rippling sparks of pleasure, the urge to keep it up hard to suppress when her damp, vaginal muscles contracted around her finger.

"Drive faster, would you?" she couldn't help asking, withdrawing her hand from between her legs and dampening her nipple with a few strokes.

"We're five minutes from the gates. Time enough to prep your other nipple for my mouth."

Screw trying to push at his control button. I'm going for the carnal decadence promised in that statement.

By the time he pulled in front of his house and cut the engine, her tenuous grip on her emotions was hanging by a thread after completing another dip into her sheath and wetting her left nipple. Without waiting for him, she opened the door and jumped down, her breasts swaying, damp nubs going rigid with the waft of summer air.

Randy strode around the truck and yanked her against him, grinding his mouth down on hers for a far-too-short kiss, the rim of his Stetson poking her forehead. Releasing her, he took her hand and hauled her inside, his urgency rubbing off on Mickie.

"I don't know which of us that little lesson tormented the most." Shutting the door behind them, he flipped the locks and continued toward his bedroom, Mickie now shamelessly relishing her exposed boobs.

The bedside lamp was turned on low, casting shadows on the walls and an amber glow across the dark-brown comforter. Without bothering to pull the covers down, he tugged her skirt off, taking her sandals with it as she stepped out. Then she was flat on her back, her blouse and bra falling to the sides as he raised her arms above her and snapped cuffs on her wrists.

Sexual excitement warred with her independent nature, annoyance with his high-handedness taking over. He looked down at her with a wicked grin, stripping off his clothes as she yanked on the restraints attached to the headboard. Ignoring the hot rush of cream her vulnerability produced, she returned his smug look with a glare.

"Let me go. I want to participate, not lie here like some pagan virgin sacrifice."

Laughing, he knelt over her hips, keeping his weight off her as he ran his hands down the sensitive underside of her arms, the same as he'd done at the club. Damn him, he knew just where to touch to throw her off track.

"Let go of me, Randy." She didn't know why she was desperate to maintain at least partial control tonight when she'd reaped such unexpected benefits from his dominance at the club.

"What's wrong?" Randy plucked at her nipples, the pinches igniting a firestorm inside her. "You didn't complain at Spurs when I bound your arms. I'm guessing that sometimes frustrating independent streak of yours is fighting against the intimacy of being in my home, in my bed. What do you think?"

He tossed out that last line as a challenge, his gaze keeping her pinned beneath him as easily as his big body. Once again, she bemoaned his astuteness that enabled him to read her with such accuracy, his attempts to get her to admit to her growing susceptibility toward this side of him taking the lead over her stubborn reluctance. The temptation of his jutting cock and glistening slit pointing upward, toward her face, making her mouth water for the taste of him didn't help. She drank in the sight of his broad chest with a sprinkling of dark, curly hair, his ripped abdominals, and thick, muscle-bulging thighs, her pulse leaping as she recalled the press of all those muscles holding her close through the night.

"I think you're full of yourself," she returned, not believing it but needing to make one last-ditch effort to keep from losing herself in him completely.

Bending his head, he kissed her then slid his mouth down to suckle each nipple in turn, his teeth nibbling, tongue soothing the tiny pinpricks. Lifting his head, he gave her one of those grins that guaranteed she was in trouble. "Still want me to let you go? Either say red, and end this, or say please. Better yet, beg me." Randy followed that ridiculous suggestion by levering himself up, shifting his knees to spread her legs wide enough to thrust two fingers with ease deep inside her pussy, exposing her aching clit for his thumb to torture.

"Damn you, Randy," she whispered, arching against his marauding hand.

A startled gasp tore from Mickie's throat as stinging, white-hot pain blossomed across the tender flesh of her labia, his sharp slap robbing her breath and rendering her speechless.

"Master Randy. Time for you to decide, Mickie. Do you want this, want me like this, or not?" He reached up with his free hand while continuing to stroke her quivering sheath and ran his fingers over the pulse in her neck. "I know you're not scared;

nothing scares you."

This does, what I'm feeling does.

"This beat doesn't lie. Are you going to?"

His tone brooked no argument, further delays, or even questions. Shaking from the need consuming her, she was left with no choice but to agree because somehow, someway, she now desired his possession above all else.

"No, you win, *Master* Randy."

"We both win, Mickie." Pulling from her grasping pussy, he scooted up until he was straddling her head, his hand wrapped around his cock, rubbing the smooth, damp crown over her lips. "Open for me."

That was an order she didn't hesitate to obey. Opening her mouth, she savored the earthy smell and taste of his hard flesh as he fed her half of his silk-covered, steely erection. Groaning, she swirled her tongue around his girth, nibbled along the throbbing veins, and sucked hard when he moved back, leaving only the mushroom cap for her to cling to with her lips. Her throat tightened as she worked to hold him inside her mouth, using her tongue to tease his slit then the sensitive area just under the rim, humming in pleasure.

"Do that again," he rasped, his face taut, etched

with the effort it must be taking him to remain in control.

"What?" she mouthed around his cock as he dipped inside her mouth again.

"That sound you made." He pulled up then thrust back once, twice, three times, and she gave him what he wanted, another purr of enjoyment. "*Fuck*, what was I thinking? Enough."

Mickie would have giggled except he yanked out of her clinging mouth to don a condom and settle between her legs then lifted them over his shoulders. With one smooth glide upward, he surged inside her with a forceful plunge, filling her with his length, stretching her muscles as she welcomed him by coating his cock with an abundance of cream.

The wanton position lifted her butt off the mattress, levering her hips at the perfect angle for his ramming strokes. "Oh God...*yes!*"

He wasn't gentle, and she surrendered to his rough, hot aggression with a low moan of answering heat, exalting in his deep, surging strokes as he set up a pounding rhythm, his breathing turning harsh against her neck. Before him, she'd been content with a night or two of sex with the few men she'd allowed that privilege. But the more she had Randy, the more she hungered for him and his demanding, possessive brand of fucking.

"Please," she whispered in his ear, tugging on her arms, aching to touch him.

"That's my girl," he crooned, panting. Reaching up, his jerking hips never slowed as he released her hands while biting the soft skin along her neck, the nips adding to the shivers running under her skin.

Mickie gripped his smooth shoulders, digging her nails into the muscles, seeking anchorage as a tidal wave of pleasure erupted in her pussy and exploded in a bright burst of spasmodic ecstasy. She rode through the intense, mind-numbing climax until it had drained every ounce of energy from her body.

Chills raced across her damp skin as Randy lowered her legs and slowly dragged his spent cock from the small, remaining clutches, her body reluctant to let him go.

"Want help into the bathroom?" he asked, rolling to his side and giving her an indulgent smile.

"No. I'm fine for now. Besides, I don't think I can move."

"I'll take that as a compliment. Be right back."

He flung the covers over her, and she eyed his firm backside as he padded into the bathroom before succumbing to a deep, sated sleep.

****

"What do you have going today?"

Randy sipped his coffee, eyeing Mickie across the small, round kitchen table. The morning sun shone in through the wide, three-paned window that offered a view of the mountains in the distance and a herd of bison grazing on summer grass. It was his favorite vista until she started living here this week, and he'd spent more time with her these past days than in the last year combined. He'd exerted so much time, effort, and soul searching after the breakup of his marriage, most of it coming to terms with the colossal mistake of marrying Melanie in the first place, he'd failed to see what was right in front of him. Not until Mickie shocked him into awareness the second she entered Spurs in a dress and heels, her blonde hair hanging loose down her back with the dim lighting picking up the red highlights, did he ever imagine she was the one for him.

"Do you mean other than loading the trucks headed to auction?" She scooped up the last bite of her third pancake soaked in syrup.

Just over fifty head of cattle were culled from the herd, having reached the prime weight to bring in top dollar. After going over the books, he was pleased with both the crop yields and cattle production, and it was still early in the year.

"Yes. I'll have time to help when the guys return before I have to leave for town and my meeting with Shawn, Dakota, and Clayton."

Mickie nodded, pushed to her feet, and carried her plate to the sink. As good as she looked in butt-hugging jeans, he wished she could wear shorts more often. He would never tire of looking at her world-class legs. Too bad shorts weren't practical for working on a ranch.

"We've got it covered. The truckers are good at helping and know what they're doing. Afterward, I'm headed into Mountain Bend also, meeting Chelsea for lunch and to run a few errands." She put her dish in the dishwasher then padded back over to the table to pick up his. "Is your meeting over club business?"

Randy circled her wrist and caressed her pulse with his thumb. "Some, plus a get-together at Rolling Hills next weekend, Sunday afternoon. Want to go?" He took the small jump in her heartbeat as a sign his invitation pleased her even though she tried to mask it with a casual shrug.

"Sure. Sounds like fun."

He let her go and stood. "We might as well ride in together. There's a storm system moving in this afternoon, and it's shaping up to be a doozy." As soon as the words were out of his mouth, he realized he phrased that wrong. Her shoulders went back, and she slammed the dishwasher door as she spun around.

"I'm perfectly capable of driving into town and back, even in the rain. Don't start trying to control my life, Randy."

That prickly attitude got his own hackles up, and he pinned her against the counter, bracing his hands behind her, and getting in her mulish face. "Don't read more into a simple, sensible suggestion, Mickie."

Her breathing hitched, her eyes going to his mouth, but she didn't back down. "I'm not taking any chances on you trying to change me into your wife, willing to do your bidding twenty-four seven, or giving you any reason to think I can be coerced in that direction."

Randy put space between them, too angry to do anything else, like give her that first spanking. Grabbing his hat off the island, he slapped it on his head, tossing her one last glare. "You conveniently seem to forget our long history, how well I know you, and I don't appreciate your lack of faith, given how well *you* know *me, baby.*"

Her eyes snapped up, a gray tempest brewing,

but he stormed out, leaving her to stew over that word, and her own words of mistrust. Instead of heading to his office to work on the never ending business side of ranching, he got in his truck and drove into town early, needing to put space between him and Mickie. He'd surprised himself, not just her when he'd pursued a change in their relationship, but unlike Mickie, he was not only willing but eager to explore a new side to their long acquaintance. And, fuck, but it had been going well until now.

Randy forced himself to recall the first time he saw her, the young, so alone kid, defiant against any attempted restraints he tried for her own safety and well-being since her parents refused the responsibility. She'd fought him every step of the way yet returned to the ranch every chance she got. He witnessed the pleasure she reaped from hanging around, tending to Black Jack, even the chores they eventually let her have a hand at trying. But despite the gratitude she had no problem showing, she wouldn't give an inch on relinquishing her independence, continuing to take off without telling anyone, returning when it suited her, giving everyone gray hairs worrying about her. She didn't know how to handle anyone caring enough to not only see she stayed safe but that she had ample to eat and constructive ways to spend her free time. He still enjoyed watching her eat with a lusty appetite, sometimes still saddened by the neglect she'd suffered before he'd paid a visit to her parents and informed them he and his family would look out for Mickie from then on, a promise and threat neither had argued about.

Parking in front of the feedstore, he cut the engine and blew out a breath, sitting a moment to get his emotions under control. The most important thing to remember in dealing with Mickie was patience, and he'd let his slip this morning. He had to remember it had only been a week since they went from buddies to lovers, and while he was ready to push for even more, she was still adjusting to his sexual control, not ready to consider a full, give-and-take committed relationship.

Grabbing his list, he switched gears and concentrated on work, leaving dealing with Mickie for later. At least coming into town early gave him the chance to get caught up on other things, and, after putting in an order at the feedstore, he went by the butcher's to arrange for pork chops for the barbeque next weekend at Rolling Hills, his contribution to the food. He was a little early arriving at the Watering Hole to meet the guys for lunch but found Clayton already seated, going over the papers laid out in front of him.

The bar was quiet with only two other tables occupied and Brandon, the bartender/owner, conversing with his cook behind the bar. Randy wound his way to the corner and took a seat, nodding to Clayton's paperwork.

"Working on a case?" When not trying someone in court where he boasted a ruthless reputation, the prosecutor was one of the easiest-going men of Randy's acquaintance. A year older than the three boys who had come to Idaho in their teens from Arizona foster care, he'd never hesitated in turning Spurs over to them when he'd needed to get away after his divorce.

"Signing off on a few depositions, working up a plea bargain." His frown indicated he wasn't happy about that negotiation.

"I've never known you to settle for anything except the strictest penalty."

"Skye talked me into going easy on this woman. Comes from an abusive home, which led to drug use. Got caught trying to rob a convenience store in Boise, wielding a knife." Clayton leaned back and shook his head. "Be careful, Randy. A committed relationship with a great woman has its merits but also its issues, like caving when she asks using a certain tone and look."

Randy gave him a rueful grin. "Mickie would just insist, no cajoling or asking nice."

Clayton raised an eyebrow. "Have you put her over your knee yet?"

"No. I have to tread more carefully than I'm used to. She wasn't in the lifestyle and is accepting it a little at a time."

"Newbies can be fun or frustrating." Shawn took the chair next to Randy and slapped him on the back. "Good luck. Dakota's tied up and can't make it."

"Problem?" Clayton asked, gathering his papers and putting them in a briefcase.

Shawn's voice hardened, along with his jaw. "Word has come down from the Coultrane's just west of here that one of their prized thoroughbreds has been stolen. They're the third breeders to fall prey to horse thieves, and we're assuming the same gang. The other two were in Wyoming and Colorado, so they're moving around."

Randy whistled. "They can get a pretty penny for Coultrane's horses, as they sell for no less than half a million. That's the last thing Adrian needs on the heels of losing his wife in that tragic cliff fall."

Adrian Coultrane and his cousin, Ashe, were regular members a few years ago, but their busy schedules had started limiting their visits.

"Any leads?" Clayton inquired.

"Not yet, but law enforcement and park rangers are on the lookout throughout the west. A couple of IT gurus are monitoring the web for black market sales that match the descriptions."

Brandon came over, pad in hand. "I'm short staffed today so I'll get your orders. Pulled pork is the special."

They made it easy for him by all three ordering the special then Clayton changed the subject to club business. After going over a few things, Randy realized what he'd been missing by not bringing in partners before selling out. A few new memberships were approved, including Mickie's – he would have to find the right way to tell her he'd taken it upon himself to get that done. He could always say it had to do with sex or mention it when he had her trembling, ready, and needy for an orgasm.

If only Randy could convince her he didn't wish to change her. He wanted her the way she was, soft, eager, and amenable when he got her naked.

****

Mickie parked down the street from Cee Cee's, the salon where her best friend Chelsea worked, and went over her list of toiletries she needed to pick up. When Randy had packed her clothes from home, he'd left out most of her personal items, not that she messed much with makeup, only the basics. She winced, thinking of him, and her uncalled-for reaction to his suggestion. Adjusting to this change was harder than she'd expected. Not the get-naked-tie-me-up part. She kind of liked that, and the orgasms she reaped from his kink.

Who would have thought? Certainly not her.

She supposed she owed him an apology, but those, too, were difficult for her. Growing up without having to answer to anyone had its merits and its pitfalls. Her teen years were spent bucking heads with Randy whenever he was around and tried to keep tabs on her. When he was gone, she got along fine with the hands and his parents, but more often than not, Steven took over for Randy, attempting to give her the parental restrictions she lacked from her mom and dad. While she resented both of them for curbing her freedom, a small part of her relished knowing their actions came from caring, a first for her.

Mickie would try to remember that going

forward with Randy. She would still make mistakes. After all, she'd never been in a relationship that was anything more than a few weeks of sex. What Randy wanted was new and exciting, yet she was on constant pins and needles wondering where it could end up, how soon before he tired of her like all the others, and she was left with no choice but to return to Colorado.

"I could sit here all day and stew or get something done," she muttered.

Grabbing her purse, she got out and started toward Casey's, Mountain Bend's small version of Walmart. Running into people she'd grown up with or knew from around town was inevitable, which made her late for meeting Chelsea after checking out. Rushing toward her truck to stash her purchases, she wasn't paying attention and ran into someone, dropping a bag.

"Sorry," she mumbled, holding out a hand for the bag he picked up before she recognized the man.

"You're..."

"You..." They spoke simultaneously.

Mickie grasped the bag and took a step back. The same man she'd come across the other day who was transporting the horse in a trailer too small for the equine's size gazed at her with a gleam of interest she didn't care for.

"Thanks. Nice seeing you again." She made to go around him, but he wrapped a hand around her upper arm, a light grip but unwelcome, nonetheless.

"I'll still be in the area another day or two. Could I talk you into joining me for dinner tonight? Somewhere of your choice. Name's Dex."

She gave his hand on her arm a pointed look, shaking her head, not about to give him her name. "Thanks, but I have plans."

To his credit, he released her right away with a sheepish grin that didn't fool Mickie or ease the same creepy vibes he gave her as the last time.

"I'm free tomorrow."

"I'm not," she returned, getting annoyed. "If you'll excuse me, I'm meeting someone."

His eyes went hard, but he smiled and tipped his hat. "Have a good day, then."

Mickie waited until he was several yards away before calling out, "I hope your horse recovered from the ride."

Dex turned, his voice laced with sarcasm as he replied, "Don't you worry your pretty head. We're taking real good care of him."

If he'd been within reach, she would have kicked his shin for that. The man was a moron and jackass. She put Dex out of her mind, stowed her purchases in the truck then hurried to the deli where she planned to meet Chelsea. Hatti, the owner, remembered everyone by name and greeted her from behind the counter as soon as she entered.

"Mickie, how nice to see you again. Is Chelsea meeting you today?"

Padding up to the counter, she returned the older woman's smile. "Your memory still amazes me, Hatti. Yes, she is. I figured she would beat me, but she must have gotten delayed." There was no one in line waiting to order, but half the tables were occupied. Reading the chalkboard on the wall, she ordered for both her and Chelsea. "We'll both take the turkey and Swiss and a brownie."

Hattie smiled. "Good to see your appetite hasn't changed. Have a seat and I'll bring it over."

Chelsea arrived as Mickie took a seat by the window. With her black hair cut in a short bob and earrings adorning both lobes along the, she appeared no older than when they were in high school.

"I thought we'd never get together." Sitting down, Chelsea cocked her head. "Okay, give, what did you do?"

"What makes you think I've done anything?" Mickie answered, stalling.

"Maybe because I know you better than anyone else, except, possibly Randy." She sucked in a breath then leaned forward with a wide grin. "You didn't. You did!" she whispered, excitement shining in her eyes. "You finally slept with him."

"What do you mean finally?" Mickie returned, pitching her voice low. Any tidbit of gossip that reached other ears was sure to get circulated by the end of the day.

"Oh, please. You two have been heading toward the sack for ages. You did confide in me after high school."

"I was a naïve ninny back then, Chels, and that mistake has nothing to do with now. It's just sex."

Chelsea patted her hand and leaned back with a smug look. "If you say so," she said as Hattie brought their order over.

"Here you go, girls. Brownie's on me."

"Thanks, Hatti." Chelsea waited until Hattie walked away before picking up her sandwich, asking, "Well, was it kinky and good, just kinky, what?"

A giggle tickled Mickie's throat and she didn't hold it back. It felt good being with her friend again. Talking long distance just wasn't the same. "Kinky, and off-the-charts good."

"You agreed to let him tie you up?" Chelsea

questioned around a mouthful.

"Yeah, can you believe it? Seriously, Chels, there's something about letting him take over that's...freeing, not to mention exhilarating. I can't explain it."

"Don't try. Go with it, enjoy it while it lasts. If he hurts you, he'll answer to me."

Mickie ate the brownie first, humming at the rich chocolate sweetness. "Damn, I love Hatti's baking. I went into this knowing his track record and won't let him hurt me. It's just sex."

Chelsea snorted. "Say that enough and you might start believing it."

Mickie already believed it. At least, that's what she told herself.

Chapter Ten

A loud thunder clap rumbled through the dark sky as Mickie waved goodbye to Chelsea and put the truck into gear. The first drops hit her windshield when she reached the highway, the sky opening up in a deluge as she neared the entrance to the trailer park. She shouldn't worry about her dad but couldn't seem to help herself. Randy, and everyone else on the ranch, had instilled the importance of responsibility on her when they'd gifted the care of Black Jack to her, followed by allowing her to help out around the stables. Her parents weren't much to brag about, but they were her only relatives.

It was hard to admit, but her mother's desertion and silence since leaving hurt. If there was a chance she could hang on to her father, she wouldn't give up on him yet, but when she noticed his car wasn't parked in front of the trailer, she realized she would have to try and reach out to him another time. She wasn't about to turn around and drive back into town and search for him at the bar, which was likely where he'd gone. The bartender never allowed patrons to drive away from the Watering Hold inebriated, making sure someone else gave them a ride, which eased her worry somewhat.

Sighing with regret as the rain turned into a downpour, Mickie got back on the main road and continued toward the ranch, wondering if she would arrive before Randy, and how she would go about making amends. The sudden tilt and hiss from a back tire, followed by the truck shifting as the tire went flat demanded her full concentration to slow down and pull over in the gusting storm. Cursing her luck, she leaned her head back, wishing the rain would let up enough for her to change the tire without drowning.

At least some luck was with her when the deluge slowed to a steady but lighter rain after five minutes. She would have to suffer the wind, but some things couldn't be helped, and she reached into the back seat for the rain slicker she kept on hand, along with a blanket and flashlight. Pulling the slicker over her head, she adjusted the hood then had to get out to shake it down to her knees.

She was alone on the road while attaching the

jack and cranking the wheel up, but before she could start working the tire off, another vehicle pulled over behind her and a tall man got out. Mickie didn't recognize him until he stopped in front of her, and she looked up and saw Dex's face, the small smile he offered doing nothing to stifle her displeasure.

"We meet again. Let me help. You can go sit in my truck."

She narrowed her eyes, pushing to her feet. "Thanks, but I've got it."

"Nonsense," he returned, his tone hardening. "Don't be stubborn and keep us both out in this rain longer than necessary."

Swiping a hand over her wet face, she blinked several times, angered by his gall. "Call me stubborn, or anything else. I don't care, just leave me alone."

Dex's somewhat congenial expression changed into a look so menacing, Mickie stumbled back. A frisson of alarm produced goose bumps as he reached one hand toward her and the other behind him, a move she recalled him doing the first time they met when he and his friend were the ones fixing a flat. The approach of another truck, which slowed to pull over, forced his hands back to his sides, and she'd never been so happy to recognize Randy's arrival as she was at that moment.

"Fine, have it your way," Dex stated, pivoting and jumping behind his wheel as Randy slid out from behind his.

Mickie's suspicions about the man rose when he tugged his Stetson lower and kept his face averted as Randy strode by his vehicle toward her.

"What's going on, kid?" he asked, his eyes on Dex's truck as he maneuvered away from the side of the road.

Given Randy's cold glare at Dex, she thought fast to defuse a potential volatile response. "Just thanking this guy for his offer of help but letting him know I've got this."

Just then, Dex took off with a spin of tires on the wet pavement, uncaring if he sent up a spray of additional water on them.

"Fuck!" Randy moved to shield her from the extra soaking, and Mickie could tell by his taut body and tone he was pissed.

Great, now I have another ticked-off male to contend with. Her day was not going well.

Striving to lighten the mood, she reminded him of her aversion to his curse. "That's not a nice word, Randy."

"Deal with it. Get in my truck, and, for once, do not argue." He glanced inside her cab and said, "I'll grab your bags and lock up. We'll take care of the tire later."

That order came seconds before a loud thunder boom heralded a fresh torrent of heavy rain, this time with the added sting of hail. Resigned to yet another confrontation before she could make up for the last one, Mickie dashed to his vehicle and breathed a sigh of relief when she shut the door. A shiver racked her body, either from being wet or from dodging a bullet with Dex, or both. No doubt about it, that man gave her the creeps, and she hoped she'd seen the last of him.

Randy's patience was wearing thin. Telling himself to give Mickie time to adjust to the changes between them wasn't working, and keeping his distance was out of the question. He grabbed her purchases out of her truck and hastened to his, cursing the hail stinging his shoulders. Jumping behind the wheel, he slammed the door, shutting out the frenzied storm. Glancing at her shivering body and seeing the wary look she cast him, the storm waging inside him wasn't so easy to close off.

"You knew I was in town. Why didn't you call and let me know about your flat?"

"You're the one who taught me how to change a

tire," she reminded him, her frown a sign she didn't understand his pissy attitude toward her.

Shaking his head, he tossed her bags in the rear then started the truck. "Yes, in case I wasn't available or within reach to help you. That wasn't the case today. Not only did you put yourself in jeopardy with the weather hindering other drivers' vision, but a lone woman stranded on the road draws the attention of jerks, like that guy."

As soon as the guy had seen Randy pulling over, he'd hightailed it to his truck, but Randy still got a glimpse of the bulge at the back of his waist. Most men in these parts owned a rifle and carried them in their vehicles, but there was no reason to go around with a concealed handgun unless they were trouble or law enforcement. He wouldn't risk Mickie by trying to confront the guy after he made the move to leave, but thinking about the danger she might have been in turned his blood to ice in his veins.

Fidgeting in her seat, Mickie turned her face toward the window as he pulled out onto the road. Hail continued to bombard the truck, the heavy rain pounding against the windshield propelled by the strong wind. Imagining her trying to change a tire under these conditions didn't help calm his rioting emotions.

"You're right. He was a jerk. He's also one of the men I saw last week changing their flat. I ran across him in town, too."

At least she was finally being open, which helped even though he didn't like the sound of that. "Did you get his name?" he asked. He didn't believe in back-to-back coincidences.

"Dex, that's all he said." Heaving a deep breath that lifted her shoulders, Mickie said, "Look, if you'll quit faulting me for being myself, I'll try harder not to piss you off."

As far as concessions went, Randy considered that generous for her. It also got him to thinking the same should apply to him. She was aware of his Dom persona long before agreeing to a scene at Spurs and shouldn't expect him to change who he was. His palm tingled imagining her draped over his lap, her white buttocks turning pink then red under his swats. With any other sub, he would deliver a punishing spanking first, followed by lighter smacks meant to calm and soothe or arouse, depending on her infraction. With Mickie, who didn't understand how her resistance to come to him with her troubles signaled she was still shy of giving this relationship her full trust, the opposite would be necessary. Her nature was to balk first, assimilate the situation second, unless he could turn the tables on her.

Stopping in the circle drive in front of the house, he replied, "Deal, as long as you give me the same consideration. Run inside."

Opening his door turned on the interior light, and he caught the flush staining her face, the flare of excitement in her eyes before she lifted her hood and sprinted inside. Randy grabbed her purchases and followed, closing and locking the front door behind him as she pulled off her slicker. Taking it, he hung it on a peg, hooking his hat next to it before setting the bags down and taking her hand.

"What are you doing, Randy?"

Mickie's breathless inquiry held a note of wariness as he led her into the great room and took a seat on the leather sofa facing the stone fireplace. "That's Master Randy," he answered, keeping hold of her hand in one of his as he undid her jeans with the other. A loud roll of thunder reverberated outside the windows as her eyes widened, the dark skies dimming the room, the driving rain hitting the glass accompanying their low voices.

"And I'm about to give you another lesson in a Dom/sub relationship. Remember the safe words and pull down your pants."

She tried stumbling back a step, but he kept

hold of her hand and she frowned. "Why?"

Randy released her hand with a scowl, leaned back and crossed his arms. "Your choices are to say red and walk away or do as I say."

She huffed, and he saw indecision cross her face, her soft mouth tightening into a familiar mutinous slash until he played dirty and cupped a hand over the tight bulge of his erection pressing against his zipper. Pure, unadulterated lust took over, and she shoved her jeans down until he stopped her at mid-thigh.

"That's good." Grabbing her wrist, he yanked her over his lap, slapping her right buttock before she could utter a protest. Her gasp ended with a low moan and slight uplift of her ass. "That's my girl," he praised her, swatting her other cheek.

With her face buried in her arms on the sofa, her voice came out muffled as she stuttered, "Randy... Master Randy, I..."

"You don't get why this" – he delivered another light spank then caressed the red spot – "is stimulating? Why you're turned on by the heat and slight discomfort?" Lifting his hand, he added a touch more force, bouncing her buttock with the next slap, taking aim at the undercurve of her right globe.

"Yes, I mean no, I don't get it." Swinging her head around, she flipped him an impish grin that came close to melting his heart. "But don't stop, *Master*."

His eyes on hers, Randy peppered her ass with a series of quick, teasing smacks, hard enough to warm and titillate, to nip but not hurt. Mickie closed her eyes, shifting her hips then laying her head back on her propped arms. Slowing his hand, he hit each undercurve again then her thighs before stopping to rub the reddened skin. She whimpered, her thighs falling apart in an unconscious invitation he accepted by skimming his fingers up the inside of one leg to her damp pussy lips.

Tracing over her slick labia, he asked, "Is this what you want, Mickie?"

"*Yes*, more." Her demand came with another enticing hip raise.

Perfect. Randy prepared for her reaction to phase two by pinning her legs down with his left leg and elevating her buttocks with a lift of his right before inflicting the next blow with more force.

The sudden pain blossoming across one cheek lifted the pleasant euphoric fog from Mickie's senses, jerking her into full awareness with a startled cry.

She tried sliding out from under Randy's punishing hand only to discover her lower half restrained by his strong leg. Her inability to free herself sent a shudder through her, or was that caused by her blood heating along with her buttocks? Swearing, confused yet aroused, she drew a hand behind her to shield her tender flesh only to have him immobilize her arm against her lower back.

"*Fudge!*" she cried out with the next sharp whack, then turned to face him again. "What... why..." Stuttering to a halt at the intense look on his face, she cringed at the censure in his dark eyes.

"You trust the only part of me you've known before entering into this relationship, but not this side of me." He spanked her two more times, hard swats that burned deep into the muscles. "I'm two sides of the same coin, Mickie. Accept it, deal with it, or use the safeword."

Mickie's pulse leaped, and her pussy wept as she sucked in a breath, working her mind around the truth of his statement and his ultimatum. Her blood had heated as fast as her butt, her cheeks throbbing under the calloused palm he laid on her abused flesh. To avoid making another mistake, she took her time assimilating what her body was saying and what her mind kept denying.

"You want me to submit to you."

"You've already done that." He proved that point by sliding his hand between her legs and thrusting two fingers inside her clutching pussy. Pulling his hand back, he lifted the glistening digits then slowly licked them, never taking his dark gaze off her face. "Your sweet pussy would be dry as a bone if you didn't need and accept what I can give you." He landed two more blistering swats then rubbed the hurt. "I not only want your *complete* trust but your willing acceptance going forward. That means confiding in me, letting me help you change a tire even though we both know you're capable of doing the task yourself."

Mickie wasn't sure she could give him what he wanted, at least not to the extent he was talking about, but damn, she wanted to try even more than she craved an orgasm at this moment. She nodded, aching inside and out. "I want that too."

Satisfaction glowed in his eyes as he squeezed one sore cheek. "If I didn't believe that going into this, I never would have gone in this direction with you. Thank you, Mickie."

The approval lacing his voice added to the slow-spreading, warm glow inside her that erupted into an inferno when he pushed her legs off the couch, stood, and knelt behind her. With urgency egging her on, she shoved her jeans down to her knees upon hearing the crinkle of a condom wrapper. The dull throbbing encompassing her backside had transferred to her empty pussy, heightening her awareness of a desperate need she'd only experienced when with Randy. Why hadn't she noticed that before? Then he was palming her cheeks, sliding his thick cock head between her labia, and she shelved further questions for later, when she could think straight.

"I love how wet you get no matter how or where I touch you," he stated in a guttural tone, spearing her pussy with one deep thrust. Leaning over her bowed back, he braced his hands on the sofa and whispered in her ear, "And the tight clutch of your welcome when I possess your sweet body." With short jabs in and out, her vaginal muscles working to cling to his girth, he drove her to the edge of orgasmic insanity within seconds, toppling her over with his next words. "Come on, Mickie, suck me dry. You're so fucking good at it. Don't make me wait."

Straightening his arms, he rammed into her over and over, forcing a mewling cry from her throat as pleasurable spasms erupted up and down her core, rippling along his steely length. Then he drew one hand downward, slipped a finger past his pummeling cock to find her clit and press the swollen nub hard against his rigid, rocking flesh. Unable to hold back against the direct, rasping stimulation, Mickie let go with another mind-numbing, body-encompassing climax that sent her drifting on a sea of pleasure as stormy as the elements raging outside.

Mickie drifted slowly back into awareness as Randy pulled from her body. The sheer decadence of kneeling there with her pants around her knees, her shirt still covering her upper body, leaving her lower half exposed for his use and enjoying the hell out of it brought home an undeniable truth. She wanted this, and him, with every fiber of her being, and would have to work harder at keeping it if she didn't want to risk blowing it.

****

Dex's brother, Chuck, flung the cabin door open and greeted his return with a terse, "Well?"

"No luck, and I tried twice." Shoving past him, Dex let his anger out by pounding his right fist into his left palm.

He was as tired and on edge holed up in this decrepit cabin as Chuck. Sitting around waiting for their buyer to make his way into the States didn't sit well with either of them, but, given the merchandise, they were at their client's mercy, not to mention his timeline.

Slamming the door, Chuck rounded on him. "We can't leave a witness behind."

"I know that," he snapped in return, glaring at his brother. "After my IT guy came through with her name from running the license plate, I followed her into town from the ranch where she works and tried luring her away with a dinner date offer. She wasn't interested, so I waited until she met a friend for lunch, rigged a slow leak in her tire, and followed her out of town. That plan was thwarted by the arrival of another motorist, so what would you have me do?"

Chuck stomped over to the beat-up refrigerator and snatched a beer from inside. Popping the cap, he downed half the can before answering. "Where's this ranch she works at?"

"South of town about twenty miles," he returned, retrieving his own can of beer.

The only good thing about the cabin they'd discovered along an upper slope while scouting for a secluded place to hang around and hide the horses was its location off the beaten, well-traversed trails. There was enough grass and foliage for the horses to graze in addition to the hay they'd stocked up on before swiping the first stallion in Montana. They stood to walk away with a tidy cash profit if they could pull this sale off without any delays.

Chuck flung himself down on a ratty chair filled with holes from mice, as if the lack of electricity and a bathroom weren't enough. "We'll take turns keeping an eye on the place, find some areas where we can watch her through binoculars, and, with luck, catch her alone, take her out quick, and get back here with none the wiser. We have two more fucking weeks before our buyer can get here and finish this."

"And he thinks he can fly the horses back to Mexico in a private jet without getting caught?" Dex asked with skepticism.

Chuck shrugged. "That's what he says, and making those plans is what's taking so long. I don't give a shit what he does with them. I just want them gone."

Dex was with Chuck there. Making sure the animals stayed in prime condition for so long under such limited conditions was trying their patience. And now they had to deal with an eyewitness to their theft.

****

Randy asked Toby to give him a ride back to Mickie's truck the next morning. He left Mickie in the shower still struggling to wake up after he'd kept her awake late last night. He'd suggested staying home tonight instead of going to the club, his goal to get her more relaxed and accepting of BDSM before they returned. Given her responses to everything he'd introduced her to, he figured she would be more receptive to public exposure by next weekend. They were attending a cookout at Rolling Hills that afternoon, which would give her more time to become better acquainted with the other girls. The timing was perfect for aiding in getting her to lower the shield she used to keep from caring too much.

"That's it up ahead." He pointed to Mickie's truck, still sitting at a tilt on the side of the road.

Toby checked for traffic then steered across the opposite lane to park facing the truck. "I'll give you a hand, save you some time."

"Thanks, appreciate it."

At least the storm had cleared out, leaving the skies a clear, cloudless blue, the morning sun warm on Randy's shoulders as he stooped to finish removing the flat. A ripple of suspicious apprehension tightened his gut when he spotted the missing air valve cap and small stone that popped off the end, an easy way to ensure a slow leak.

"Son of a bitch," he swore, pushing to his feet.

"What's up?" Toby peered at the tire, his brows dipped in a frown.

"Ever heard of a stone getting wedged in a capless valve on its own?"

"That's impossible."

Randy shifted his gaze to look at Toby. "Exactly."

Fury turned the younger man's face rock hard. "Someone pulled a dangerous prank on Mickie?"

Either that, or she picked up a stalker when she turned down that man yesterday. "It looks that way. Don't say anything to anyone until I talk to her, please."

"Sure. We'll keep an eye out for anything else for a while in case it wasn't random. I'd hate to see her get hurt."

"Me and you both, Toby. Let's get this done."

Randy turned his head as the girls' laughter reached them at the corral, and he was glad he'd opted to hold off until after the cookout to talk to Mickie about the tire and the guy she'd turned down yesterday who had also, coincidentally, arrived in time to help her. He loved seeing her so relaxed and having fun, enjoying herself with Lisa, Skye, Poppy, Amie, and Jen. His friends had chosen well, settling down with women who seemed perfect for them, unlike his poor choice in Melanie. More than her infidelity, the mistake in believing he couldn't be happy with anyone for the long term who didn't possess a deep need for twenty-four seven submissiveness still stuck in his craw.

The truth of what and who he really wanted was right before him all along. He had found himself willing to accept and embrace this surprising development between him and Mickie more than she, which didn't come as a surprise given her upbringing. Regardless of the years he and his family had taken her under their wing, or how many ways they tried to show her acceptance and caring, she still held a part of herself back. She was too used to going her own way without relying on anyone or expecting others to care enough to always be there for her.

The way Mickie had received his harsher, punishing swats with stoic forbearance then splintered apart from his rough possession proved her sexual desire for his dominance, a fact she hadn't denied or shied away from all weekend. If only he could be as successful in convincing her he wanted her for the long haul, for more than an affair. She still showed a wary reluctance to discuss their affair as anything except a temporary change between them.

"Can you take your eyes off your girl long enough to give me an answer, Daniels?"

Randy swung around and nudged his Stetson to look at Dakota with amusement, unperturbed by his friend's growl. Dakota snarled a lot but had a heart of gold. "I seem to remember a trip home for your reception and saying something similar when you couldn't pull yourself away from Poppy's side," he drawled, leaning his forearms on the fence.

Dakota crossed his massive arms in a belligerent stance. "She was still recovering from her bone marrow transplant. Do you want the filly or not?"

The coal-black foal romped around the corral with her dam, one of Dakota's stunning Morgans. His venture into horse breeding this past year had already paid off with buyers placing holds on the first offspring. Randy had been touched when Dakota offered this filly as a welcome-home gift after he'd inquired about purchasing one for Mickie.

"You know I do, but remember, not a word to Mickie yet. She's a surprise for her birthday. As much as I appreciate the offer, I'd like to pay you something for her. I don't want the guilt of giving away a gift."

"Buy me dinner on prime rib night at the restaurant, stow the guilt, and we'll call it even." Slapping him on the back, Dakota said, "Shawn's waving us over, and I'm starving. Let's eat."

There was no arguing with Dakota, so he gave up. "I'm all for that."

Satisfied with the arrangement and grateful for friendship, Randy fell in step with him, walking toward the back patio where Shawn, Clayton, Ben, and Drew were gathered around the grill. He'd missed cookouts such as this one during the year he'd wasted licking his wounded pride over his failed marriage. The six of them were friends since high school, but their mutual interest in Spurs ten years later had brought them all closer together. He should have remembered that and trusted in getting their support without judgement.

It wasn't a short hike back up to the farmhouse, but the warm afternoon and slight breeze made for a pleasant stroll. After growing up experiencing harsh Idaho winters, he never passed up a chance to enjoy the outdoors in the warmer months.

As he approached, Mickie glanced at him from where she sat at the picnic table, one leg bent and tucked under her butt. She wore shorts, her hair in its usual braid, and a sleeveless blue tank top that bared her tanned, toned arms and draped over her small breasts. The skinny, gangly kid had developed into an attractive woman, her arms and legs rounding out and shaping nicely, her breasts the perfect size for her slender body even though she didn't think so.

Blood rushed to his dick, and he found himself craving that delectable body with an edgy, intense surge of lust. Too bad there were ranch hands working close enough to negate turning this get-together into a play party.

"Shit, Randy, get a grip already," Clayton said, the twinkle in his blue eyes a sign he was teasing.

"Nah, more fun to drag her into the woods on the way home," he returned, grabbing a beer out of the cooler.

Shawn lifted a brow. "Public exposure is against the law."

Randy shrugged. "That only adds to the spice."

Ben smirked. "Don't let him fool you, Randy. He's not above bending those laws for certain reasons."

"Are we headed inside after dinner?" Drew wanted to know.

"Can't." Shawn shook his head with regret, scooping the pork chops off the grill and onto a platter. "We have a Skype session planned with

Father Joe shortly."

"Saved by the priest," Clayton quipped.

"He's probably going to ream us for not calling last week." Dakota used prongs to stack potatoes on the plate Clayton held.

"He'll understand our busy schedules. He always does." Shawn led the way over to the table the girls already set with plates and silverware, a large salad placed in the center.

"Does your priest know about Spurs?" Mickie asked, scooting over to make room for Randy as he took the seat on the end next to her.

"Sure. We don't keep things from him. He doesn't judge." Clayton squeezed in between Skye and Lisa.

"Just lectures," Dakota grumbled.

Poppy flipped him a quick grin. "You should be used to that. I'm forever lecturing you to quit acting so overprotective."

Everyone around the table chuckled. "Good luck with that," Drew told her.

Spending down time with friends again helped Randy set aside his worry about the man who might or might not be harassing Mickie in a dangerous way until they went inside. Mickie followed him, but he didn't notice her pausing by the kitchen table where

Shawn had left an open folder until her surprised comment drew everyone's attention.

"I know this man." She pointed to a photo and looked over at Randy. "This is Dex, the same guy I saw last week, hauling the horse trailer, and again yesterday."

Chapter Eleven

Mickie grew uncomfortable when Shawn and Randy's faces darkened as both men strode to the table, crowding her between them. "Which one, Mickie?" Shawn wanted to know, spreading out the other photos.

"This one." She again pointed to Dex, positive of her identification. Then she saw the three photos of stunning prize horses, one of them a very pale gray similar to the glimpse she'd gotten of the horse Dex and his friend had been hauling.

Randy, with his astuteness, asked, "What else are you recognizing?"

By then, Dakota, Clayton, Ben, and Drew had joined them at the table, their faces reflecting expressions just as tight as Shawn and Randy's. Pinpricks of uneasiness crawled under her skin, and her voice came out sharper than she intended. "What's going on?"

"His name is Dex Carbello, and this" – Shawn slid a photo forward of the other man Mickie had seen that first day – "is his brother, Chuck. They're persons of interest in the recent thefts of these stallions." He gestured to the pictures of the horses.

Mickie frowned. "Wouldn't microchips make it almost impossible to get away with that, especially in stallions like these that are worth, what, close to a million?"

Dakota lifted a midnight brow, clearly impressed with her insight. Randy shrugged, his praise easing the chills giving her goose bumps as he replied, "My girl knows horseflesh."

"Good question, Mickie," Clayton said with a wink. "But if they can find an unscrupulous veterinarian to remove the chips, that's half the battle of passing the stolen equines into the buyer's possession."

Randy drew her attention back to his inquiry. "Did you see Dex with one of these horses when you came across him last week?"

"I can't be sure because they had him in a cramped trailer, but the glimpse I could get of his coat was this color." She indicated the pale horse then pointed to the picture of Chuck Carbello. "He was also there."

"Fuck."

She flicked Randy a censuring glare. "That's not..."

"Yeah, yeah, not a nice word. Tough, this isn't a nice situation. There's no way you bumped into him in town the other day by accident, and he sure as hell didn't happen upon you with your flat by coincidence." He lifted stormy eyes over her head and told Shawn in a clipped tone she didn't care for, "We need to talk."

"Not without me." She wasn't about to let him run roughshod over her.

Mickie could see him struggling to rein in the urge to go all caveman on her and gave him time to remember she wasn't his malleable wife. When he released a frustrated sigh, she let go with her pent-up breath. She really didn't want a confrontation in front of everyone.

"Give us a few minutes to discuss this then we'll talk on the way home. Deal?"

As far as compromises, she couldn't find fault with his offer even though she preferred he let her in on everything sooner than later. From the looks on the other guys' faces, she was lucky to get that.

"Fine." Without another word, she went out back and threw herself onto the glider, pushing it with her toes and crossing her arms as she stewed.

The door opened again, and the girls came out, glancing at her with both sympathy and support. Poppy brushed her arm as she settled next to her. "They're overbearing and overprotective, more so with us because they care. It helps to deal with them if you remember that."

Amie smiled, plopping down on the picnic table bench. "I'm still adjusting, and I've been with Ben since last fall, but have to admit, the benefits of loving a dominant man make putting up with those traits more than worthwhile."

"I like Shawn's overprotectiveness. It saved my life." Lisa gestured toward Skye and Amie. "You two have to admit, Clayton and Ben were there for you also."

"I'll never forget how he confronted the two women responsible for upending my life, and how his overbearing behavior helped to keep me from sinking into a deep depression when my mother's death came so fast afterward," Skye admitted.

"But that doesn't mean they let their guys walk all over them twenty-four seven," Jen put in. "You just have to learn to pick your battles, Mickie."

Mickie let the tension slip from her muscles, grateful for their insight, support, and advice. "This is all so new, and I keep thinking I'm nothing like Randy's wife, which makes me wonder why he wants me."

"I knew Melanie, and always thought her manipulative, despite her desire to submit completely. Her deceit might be why Randy is trying a different type of relationship with you, using you as a diversion while he gets over the final dregs of his anger and hurt," Jen said with a bluntness Mickie was grateful for. "Or Melanie's actions opened his eyes to what and who he really wanted. I don't envy you the position he's put you in, but, like you, I've known him since we were young. In my opinion, you won't find a better guy if it works out between you."

The guys came out just then, and Randy forestalled any further comments from Mickie as he took her hand and tugged her to her feet. "Thanks for the invite today. I'll get back to you, Shawn."

She didn't argue when he headed toward the vehicles out front, instead waving to everyone and calling out, "Thanks. It was fun." As soon as he started the engine, though, she snapped on her seatbelt, ready for him to fill her in.

"Here's the thing, kid. If the brothers are caught without the horses, you're the only person standing between them and prison." He pulled out onto the highway, flicking her a quick glance.

Well, *duh.* "I already figured that out, but don't you dare tell me I can't leave your house, or your side until they're found. The ranch, *your* ranch runs smoothly on hard work, not by itself."

Randy slowed then stopped to allow a moose and her calf to cross. His forearm muscles rippled as he clenched his hands on the steering wheel. She could read him almost as well as he could her, and she appreciated his effort to refrain from giving her orders. Because she wasn't stupid and realized the danger she could be in, she met him halfway.

"I won't leave the ranch without you, and I won't go anywhere on it without you or one of the hands. They always have their rifles when we're on the range, and I'll start carrying mine." She sent him a smug look. "You know I'm a crack shot since you taught me."

Lifting his Stetson, he raked a hand through his hair, scraping the thick waves back before settling his hat back on and tugging the rim low. He hit the gas after the moose were across and disappearing into the woods before saying, "Hell, you're better than a few of them. Okay, Mickie. You're right. We both have to work. We've got crops coming in and others that need sowing, not to mention tending the livestock. Our ranch might be one of the smaller ones, but it's still large enough to keep ten hired hands on the payroll this time of year. Stick close to the barns as much as possible."

****

Other than her parents, Mickie had never lived with anyone before last week when Randy had returned from her dad's with her bags packed. She'd spent too much of that time adjusting to and wallowing in his sexual demands to give it much thought. With the threat against her causing him to hover to the point of distraction and annoyance, it was taking every ounce of her willpower to keep from snapping at him every time she turned around and found him breathing down her neck.

Okay, she conceded, standing under the multiple shower jets spewing hot water down her body from head to toe, front and back, she could really get into his pampering, his way of appeasing the chafing she was experiencing from the necessary restrictions. Every night, after they fixed dinner then did the dishes together, he made popcorn and rubbed her feet while they watched a movie. The soothing massage went a long way each evening to ease her taut nerves and frayed temper. By the end of the show, his hands were sliding up her bare legs, eliciting tingles of anticipation that stirred her from the relaxed stupor his deep-tissue foot massage had induced.

The man's creativity in coming up with different ways to restrain her around the house and wring powerful orgasms from her straining body also made the tenseness of having her freedom curbed more bearable. Her favorite thus far was having her wrists bound to her upper thighs while he pressed her against the windows, her nipples rubbing up and down the glass as he took her from behind. Then there was his sadistic side, which she still couldn't figure out why she responded to just as strongly when he tormented her in what should be an unpleasant manner, like last night. He'd gone and ruined the lovely soft pulses across her buttocks from a long, over-the-knee spanking in the stable by flipping her off his lap onto the haystack to suffer the scratchiness abrading her tender skin. Her cheeks clenched as she recalled the deep, two-fingered anal thrusts that accompanied his driving cock into her pussy.

Sometimes, the good and what shouldn't be good aspects of this relationship were hard to separate.

The bathroom door opened, and Mickie blinked water out of her eyes to look over the marbled half wall and see Randy leaning against the sink counter with his arms crossed, a crooked smile playing around his mouth.

"You could knock," she grumbled for form, not at all put out by his blatant ogling.

"I could, but this is more fun. I do enjoy looking at you."

Mickie's heart continued to pitter-patter every time he talked to her in that slow, sexy drawl. "Are you going to join me so I can indulge in the same pleasure?" she asked, swiping her wet hair off her face.

"Unfortunately, I don't have time," he replied, coming forward and grabbing a towel off the warming rack.

Disappointed, she turned the water off and stepped into the towel he held open. "*Mmm*, I love your gadgets." She sighed and leaned into him as he dried her off, relishing another example of his pampering.

Skimming a broad palm under the towel, he cupped one buttock, squeezed, then pressed her bare mound against his rough, denim-covered erection.

"And I love your reaction to them, and me." With a low laugh, he whipped the towel off her and slapped her butt, hard. "Get dressed. I gotta get going."

Rubbing the burn, she glared at his retreating back. "Where?" She'd quit asking why as he rarely offered explanations, unlike when she was younger.

"Out to Rolling Hills to meet with Shawn. I won't be gone long." He left the bathroom door open and disappeared into the walk-in closet.

Mickie hurried to yank on her jeans and tank top, tucking it in as she came out of the bathroom. "Would you do me a favor and check on Dad while you're out?" Sitting on the chair, she pulled on her boots, trying to read his expression when he walked out of the closet.

"He doesn't deserve your concern, but, yes, if you want. But only because I don't want you taking off to do it on your own."

"Hey!" Mickie pushed to her feet, fisting her hands on her hips. "All week, for five long days, I've worked inside or around the stable yards, not complaining about one or more of the guys glued to my side." He stared her down, and she huffed. "Okay, not much, and I'm not dumb enough to take off alone."

Randy took two steps and drew her close for

a hug followed by one of his toe-curling, pussy-dampening kisses. Lifting his head, he said, "Thank God for that," then released her to take her hand. "I have time for a cup of coffee with you before I go. Is Jen still coming out for lunch?"

"Yes, so quit worrying. I'll be with someone the whole time you're gone."

She didn't mention Jen was loaning her something from her fetish wardrobe to wear to the club tonight. Randy had sacrificed the most to try and make this work between them, and she was starting to believe his feelings were stronger than she'd first thought. It was time she admitted how much she wanted him and this change between them to last, and that meant making more of an effort to give in to his desires tonight.

Mickie almost went giddy from the hot rush of expectation when she imagined surprising him for a change.

The last thing Randy wanted to do after the dead-end meeting with Shawn was deal with Ed Taylor. The lack of leads in finding the Carbello brothers wasn't Shawn's fault. After coming close to losing Lisa to a stalker, the sheriff, like Randy, was leaving nothing to chance. But even with all the effort from law enforcement and park rangers, he still chafed at the delay that kept Mickie in danger.

Driving to the trailer park, he couldn't help wishing she wasn't so admirably loyal to her parent. Every time he had arrived to pick her up at the poorly kept mobile home and witnessed an argument between her parents or seen a stricken look on her face as she dashed out the door before he could come inside, it had taken herculean effort to keep from laying into them. Mickie had been at her most difficult to keep track of on those days, leaving him no choice but to assign one of the hands to watch out for her.

If there were ever two people who shouldn't have had a child, it was the Taylors. His chest tightened at that thought, and how much Mickie had impacted his life, both in the past and since his return. Maybe her folks *shouldn't* have subjected a child to their toxic relationship, but he was damn glad for that error in their judgement. It had taken him too long to realize the child he had taken under his wing and cared for had matured without losing her ability to annoy and challenge him yet drawing his highest regard for what she could accomplish against all odds.

Rapping on the trailer's front door, Randy

decided he was hanging onto Mickie, and woe to anyone who tried to take her from him.

Ed flung the door open with an unfriendly glare, but at least he appeared sober, clean-shaven, and for once, dressed in neat, laundered clothes. "Where's my daughter?" he demanded with a belligerent thrust of his chin.

"While I can't say it's nice to see you again, Taylor, I have to admit you're looking better." He lifted his eyes over the older man's head and could see enough inside to note another positive change in the tidiness.

"She's not with you?"

Randy gave him credit for the minor changes even if he doubted they would last or Mickie's absence had anything to do with them. "No, but she asked me to check on you. I see you're fine, so I'll be on my way."

"I want to see her," Ed insisted with a lift of his chin that reminded Randy of Mickie.

The hint of desperation in the older man's hostile tone gave him pause but not enough to add to Mickie's stress. "No. She has enough to deal with after coming face-to-face with horse thieves. Cleaning yourself up doesn't atone for what you did, or the years you didn't give a shit about her."

Dismissing Ed's stricken look, his mood turned even more sour when he arrived at the house and saw Melanie's sporty Mustang parked out front. The last he'd seen of his ex, she was leaving the house with the bags he had packed for her. Before taking off, it was rumored she'd wasted no time moving in with the boyfriend in Boise. Her gall at showing up here unannounced surprised him given their harsh words when they parted.

Struggling to hold onto his temper, he stormed inside, cursing himself for not changing the locks last year. He found her making herself at home behind the corner bar in the den, her back to the afternoon sun streaming in the windows.

"Help yourself, why don't you?" Leaning against the arched entry into the room, he crossed his arms and glared in frigid welcome.

"Master," she breathed in her soft voice, her blue eyes drinking him in before she gulped down a swig of whiskey. "It's good to see you."

"I can't say the same. Why are you here, Melanie?"

He could tell she was expecting a much friendlier reception. Why, he couldn't imagine, but then, she always thought highly of herself and her appeal.

Melanie lifted the bottle, this time filling the glass halfway, then walked around the bar. He took in the thigh-skimming sundress, her braless breasts clinging to the soft, stretchy material, nipples erect from whatever fantasy was weaving through her head. Her face suffused with pleasure and a touch of satisfaction as he came forward. He hated the reminders of what a fool he'd been.

Melanie lifted a hand to his cheek and went on her toes to kiss him. When he didn't take over and claim her mouth, she stepped back with a look of sorrow. "I deserved that, I know, but I realized a few months ago what a huge mistake I made, Master Randy, and how good you were for me. Do you think you can forgive me?"

"Funny," he drawled, tossing his hat onto the sofa, "it didn't take me nearly that long to come to my senses. Since you did me a favor, there's nothing to forgive, baby, so back off and see yourself out." He plucked the glass from her hand at the rare show of anger crossing her face.

Instead of heeding the warning in his voice, her hands went to the thin straps of her dress. "Come on, Master Randy, please give me a second chance. I admitted I made a mistake, and I'll accept whatever punishment you deem fit, here or at the club or both."

Randy didn't want a scene any more than he wanted Mickie to return and get the wrong idea. Setting his jaw, he tugged the straps back up before she bared her breasts then pushed her hands aside as she reached toward him. "You set me free to discover our entire marriage was a mistake, so we'll call it even. There are no second chances, no going back."

Melanie clenched her hands into fists, her face turning bright red. "You're just going to throw away all those years, our life together that was so good for both of us?"

"You can't hear the hypocrisy of your own words, can you?" He shook his head, wishing he could get those years back. "They were years we both wasted on the wrong person, and I intend to make up for lost time as fast as I can. Maybe you should do the same."

He reached for her elbow, but she jerked away with a sneer. " You're fucking that little tomboy, aren't you? I heard about you two hooking up from some friends at the club."

Randy's impatience edged into fury. Gripping her chin, he got in her face and ground out, "She might be a tomboy in your narrow view, but Mickie is more woman than you'll ever be. Now get the hell out of my house."

At least Melanie still recognized when she'd pushed him too far and snatched her purse off the chair. He didn't bother asking for the key back as he didn't trust she hadn't already made a copy. He would change the locks first thing.

Mickie entered the den, and Randy tensed, but when she stepped aside to let Melanie pass and did nothing more than send her off with a taunting finger wave and smile, he relaxed. "So," she said, cocking her head, "shall we start dinner? I need time to shower and change before we leave for Spurs."

If he didn't already know he loved her, the sucker punch to his gut would have driven that realization home. Maybe his love for the kid had taken its time growing into the deep, soul encompassing feelings he harbored for the woman she'd become, but regardless of the mistakes made on the way to this point, there was no going back. And he would make damn sure she eventually agreed, no matter how long it took.

"Now that you mention it," Randy said, cupping her face and drawing her against him, "I am starving." He kissed her, letting her know it wasn't just food he hungered for.

After dinner, he gave Mickie thirty minutes to do what she needed in the bathroom, waiting for her to finish to see how she would react to something new. Then again, he thought, taking the strand of pink anal beads out of the package, maybe she had experimented with toys. It was never a good idea to discuss previous lovers, and given the possessive displeasure that tightened his abdominal muscles if he imagined her with someone else, he thought it best to remember that.

The bathroom door opened and the second his eyes landed on her, a ravenous hunger to stake his claim dug painfully into his balls. Seeing her dressed in an electric-blue leather mini skirt that hugged her hips and upper thighs and matching demi bra that shelved the plump undersides of her breasts, propping up her nipples, he almost swallowed his tongue in surprise. Given the gleam in her pewter eyes, he suspected that had been at least part of her intention.

"Where did you get that outfit?" Randy crooked a finger at Mickie, beckoning her over to where he stood by the bed. When she halted in front of him, he noticed her struggled breathing and erect nipples.

"Jen loaned it to me." She shrugged, as if it was no big deal. "When in Rome, and all that."

"I like the way you're thinking, Mickie. Hold onto that thought." Running a finger back and forth across one puckered tip, he said, "It appears we were on the same page tonight with clothing."

She lifted a hand to trace his nipple through the thin black mesh separating the short leather sleeves from the center leather insert of his snug-fitting T-shirt tucked into black jeans. "And here I thought I would surprise you."

"Oh, make no mistake, Mickie, you did. Does your outfit mean you're more receptive to me taking you further tonight?"

"Let's say I'm willing to try, for you."

He wasn't dumb enough to waste time questioning her about that statement or reading too much into those few words. "In that case, bend over the bed." Holding up the six beads that ranged from small to large, he watched her eyes widen with wariness. "Haven't used these before? They're made of smooth marble, easy to roll. You'll barely notice them if you're not moving."

She looked doubtful but said, "If you say so."

"That's my girl," he murmured, pressing between her shoulders to remind her of his instructions.

She bent at the waist, bracing on her elbows,

her thighs tensing as he worked the tight skirt up and moved the narrow thong strap bisecting her buttocks to the side. Rubbing one cheek, he waited until she relaxed to lube her ass with two greased fingers before inserting the string of beads, small end first.

Mickie groaned, shifting her hips as he pushed the fifth one past the tight resistance of her anus. "One more. Deep breath." As soon as she inhaled, he embedded the last, largest ball, leaving the looped end hanging out for easy removal. "Done. Not so bad, is it?" he asked, assisting her up and tugging the skirt back down.

"Not now. I'll let you know later," she returned with a cute dip in her slim brows as she assimilated the sensations.

"Good enough. Let's go."

Randy lifted her into the truck, and she released another low groan with the pressure on her ass. Without commenting, he slid behind the wheel and started out, the first big bump eliciting a sharp curse on a hiss.

"Shit!"

"Problem?" he asked, injecting as much innocence in his voice as possible.

"They're not exactly comfortable," she griped,

and he imagined the rolling shifts from the different size balls were even more acute.

"You didn't say that when I put them in."

Mickie punched his shoulder, reminding him of her strength. "I wasn't sitting on the damn things, which I'm sure you know."

She might be amendable to Randy pushing her tonight, but she would never be putty in his hands. God, he loved her.

Chapter Twelve

"God damn it!"

Dex pounded his palm on the steering wheel, watching the witness to their theft drive down the road with the fucking cowboy who had been sticking to her like glue. From what he could observe perched in different, hidden locations using binoculars, when he wasn't with her, one or more of the cowhands took his place. Either they suspected something, or they were all overprotective pansies. Either way, it made getting to her impossible, and the delay put him and his brother at higher risk of getting caught.

To make matters worse, their buyer wanted the merchandise sooner rather than later, forcing their hand. Couldn't one fucking thing go right? He pulled out of the copse of trees across the road and field from the entrance to the Daniels' ranch and drove back to the old logging trail that led to the cabin. It had taken considerable time and effort using the limited Internet connection in the mountains to research the area where the woman had first surprised them, riding out of the forest along that back road where they were changing the flat. After discovering they'd been traveling so close to a busy, working ranch, it had only taken a few discreet inquiries at gas stations to get the gossip on the Daniels and the blonde who worked for them.

If for nothing else, small towns were good for garnering information through gossip. Too bad the flat Dex had arranged for Ms. Taylor hadn't paid off. Snatching her from the same mishap as the flat that made it possible for her to upend their plans would have been sweet revenge.

He returned to the cabin and went inside, bracing for Chuck's wrath. Before his brother could ask, Dex said, "Snatching her will be impossible."

Chuck glared then grabbed a beer from the refrigerator. After downing half of the can in one long swallow, he snapped, "Fine. We take her out from a distance, and anyone who gets in our way. We'll take up different posts, anywhere we can find a good place that gives us an expanded view of the ranch without being seen, then find a way to lure her to those areas."

"Given our luck, the chances of getting away clean aren't good," Dex pointed out. If it weren't for the profit that would set them up for life, he would walk away and cut his losses.

"Better than leaving an eyewitness behind."

Yeah, there was no arguing that. If they could get through the weekend, they would be home free and on their way to a nice warm island to live a life of leisure.

****

Every move, every small bump in the road shifted the balls inside Mickie's rectum. The way they rolled along sensitive nerve endings she'd never imagined lined that orifice produced goose bumps along her arms. The waist-length, short-sleeved, bright pink wrap she wore over the demi bra did little to disguise the pinpoints of her propped-up nipples. To keep from dwelling on entering the club in the exposing, risqué outfit with a riot of sensations bombarding her body, she turned to Randy and asked about her dad.

"Was Dad okay when you saw him earlier?"

She couldn't read his expression in the dark and with his hat obscuring his eyes, but at least his tone was neutral and not angry when he replied,

"Yes. He wants to see you, and he looked better than I've ever seen him, if that helps ease your mind."

"It does, thank you." Her dad's startling, unexpected abuse still rankled and hurt, but she attributed it to the stress of her mother's desertion and his constant back pain. Randy would insist that was no excuse, and maybe he would be right, but she couldn't bring herself to give up on the only family left to her. "Once this guy is caught, I'll go by and see him."

He sighed, and she knew he didn't understand. Before he could say so, she explained the best she could. "There were times before I met you I would get scared, wondering what would happen to me, where I would go if they didn't want me anymore or something bad happened to them. We have no extended family that I know of. When I wasn't taking off to get away from the arguing, I did everything I could to make myself useful to them." Feeling his acute attention, she shrugged, as if that was no big deal. "Old habits are hard to break."

Randy reached over and squeezed her hand, the simple gesture warming her as much as when he said, "You have me now, more than ever, and an extended family. Feel free to wash your hands of both of them."

"Randy," she chided. He was raised better than to think that way. "He's still my dad, and until he proves irredeemable, I have to be there for him. I can't give up hope."

He was quiet for a minute as he parked. "Don't take this wrong, but, *baby*, you're one in a million."

Mickie's first inclination was to stiffen and lay into him, but he jumped out and shut the door, giving her the seconds she needed to produce a smile when he came around and lifted her down. "You did that on purpose to distract me."

"You always were a smart girl."

Over the years, Randy had been generous with his praise but never spared her criticism or lectures either, telling her both were necessary to learn. She'd struggled accepting both growing up, not used to anyone caring enough to bother. Odd how she liked that combination applied to this sexual lifestyle she was still adjusting to. In the last two weeks, the approval in his voice generated a warm fuzzy, helped her relax; the instructions and reprimands relieved her from having to think about anything except listening to what was expected or what to do next. She was counting on that to hold her in good stead tonight when she pushed herself past her comfort zone, hoping to please him for a change.

Randy hung his hat on a hook inside the foyer then turned to slip the light cover off her shoulders. The cooler air drew her exposed nipples into tighter nubs, but it was the sheer decadence of entering the crowded space already exposed and aroused that suddenly made her uncomfortable. The last time she was here, Randy's hands and mouth were all over her as he'd stripped and restrained her, the shocking arousal his touch produced erasing the embarrassment of public exposure. She sucked in a breath, determined not to turn wimpy because a few eyes were following them as he led her toward the bar. When he hoisted her onto a barstool and winked, stroking a finger over each nipple, she went wet and happy, her uncharacteristic timidity disappearing as fast as it had hit her upon entering.

Nick strolled over to them from behind the bar, but with Randy pressing so close to her, she didn't mind the other man's blatant look. "Good to see you again, Mickie. A light beer, same as last time?"

"Yes, Sir, thank you." This week, it seemed easier to remember the rule of addressing the Doms with a polite deference. Or maybe it was easier because the bartender was as hot as Randy even though his gaze on her breasts didn't affect her the same as when Randy leveled his hot eyes on her.

"Any news?" Nick asked Randy as he reached for a glass under the bar.

"No, but not from a lack of effort. There's a three-state manhunt for them."

Perching on the stool next to hers, Randy laid a hand on her bare thigh, his thumb sliding toward the inside and making slow circles. Heat curled low in Mickie's belly, the temptation to spread her legs hard to stifle. She prayed they didn't chitchat long as she could use that cold beer.

"Good. They'll get them. It's only a matter of time." Nick lifted a finger, indicating he'd be right back, and strode down to the cold storage to retrieve two bottles then returned and poured one in the glass, handing it to her then passing the bottle to Randy before leaning on his elbows on the bar top. "I worked with some of them over the years when I was on the force in Cheyenne."

"You were a cop?" Randy sounded surprised. "What made you leave?"

A closed expression came over the bartender's face, but Mickie was too distracted by Randy's wandering fingers up her thigh to do more than listen with half an ear.

"I was ready for a change." Straightening, he said, "Flag me down if you need anything else."

"He doesn't talk about his former profession," Neil said, joining them at the bar.

Mickie marveled at how fast she'd adapted to other men openly eyeing her bare breasts, but when Ben's eyes wandered down to her thigh where Randy was driving her nuts with his teasing caresses, she struggled not to fidget. Clenching her buttocks didn't help as that only served as a reminder of the balls stuffed up her butt.

"I noticed that. Have any idea why?" Randy wrapped his arm around her waist and tightened, the snug hold helping her to relax.

Neil shook his head. "No, not a clue. We all have skeletons in our closet, though, so no one has pushed him to open up. According to Clayton, who approved his application, his reputation at a club in Wyoming is impeccable, and that's all that matters."

"I agree. Maybe he'll find what he's looking for here, like I did."

Randy nipped her earlobe, the sharp prick as pleasurable as his open acknowledgement of his feelings. She was inching closer and closer to believing this could be more than an affair, that he wanted her in a way that went beyond his previous relationships.

Neil looked at Randy in silent inquiry, her

abdomen knotting with suspicion when Randy nodded against her head. Mickie wasn't prepared for Neil to circle a nipple and lean down to brush a soft kiss across her lips, or for her body to respond with a lightning flash of heat that released a spate of cream between her legs. Confused by her reaction when Randy was the only one she wanted, she took a long drink of the cold brew as Neil walked off without a word. Lowering her glass, she turned questioning eyes up to him.

"Is sharing one of your preferences?"

"If it is?" he asked without answering.

What woman didn't fantasize about having two men? Even so, she wasn't keen on the idea but remembered her resolve to concentrate on pleasing him. "I came tonight intending to fit in, so if that's what you want."

He frowned, and she couldn't figure out why he disapproved of that. Keeping his eyes on hers, he slid the hand on her thigh upward and one finger under her thong to delve between her labia. Then he had the audacity to hold up his wet finger, and she didn't know whether to get pissed, embarrassed, or excited.

"Were you this aroused before Master Neil touched you? Be honest."

Heeding the warning in his tone, Mickie gave him a blunt, honest answer. "I've been aroused since I saw your reaction to my outfit. Having others look, Master Neil's brief touch, added to what you started, but what I..." she paused, floundering for the right word.

"Need?" he supplied for her. "I don't want you submitting to anything just to please me."

Taking the glass from her hand, he raised the arm braced around her waist, shifting her upper body until his arm rested on his thigh and she lay looking up at him. Lifting the glass, he sent shock waves through her when he trickled the cold beer onto her upturned breasts and nipples.

Mickie didn't pay any attention to the people seated nearby or standing around the bar. The low beat of music didn't resonate past the roaring in her head as he dipped down to lick her tingling flesh and suckle her nipples, her pelvis jerking, her thighs falling open to give him easy access for his returning fingers. She convulsed with pleasure, perspiring from the inferno his touch ignited. Before her building climax could erupt, he pulled back and lifted her upright, positioning her to stand between his legs.

Gripping his shoulders to maintain her wobbly

balance, she strove to get herself under control, to keep from snapping in frustration. Taking a fortifying breath, she asked, "What do you want, *Master* Randy?" He clasped her hips as she made to step back, the move stirring the anal beads again and adding to the hypersensitivity consuming her body.

There was no mistaking the reprimand in his voice as he answered, "Only for you to be yourself, Mickie."

Relieved yet put out he was rebuffing her intention to give back some of what he'd gifted her with, Mickie forgot the rules and snapped, "Fine. Then start with getting this damn thing out of my butt."

Uh, oh.

Randy's mouth tightened as he pushed away from his perch on the barstool. "By all means."

Mickie gasped as he spun her around and pushed between her shoulders until she lay with her breasts flattened on the bar top. Grasping her wrists, he shackled both in one hand, held them behind her, shoving her skirt up with the other. The sharp, painful blows covering each buttock stole her breath.

"I...didn't mean *here*!" she huffed, conscious

of the eyes that must be on her bared butt with the protruding loop attached to the row of beads.

"You should have thought of that before using that tone." He tugged on the loop, removing the first, largest ball. "Being yourself means don't agree to something because you think it will please me, which you should know." Another two smacks burned her cheeks. "It doesn't mean giving me attitude for putting your needs and pleasure before mine."

She never thought of it that way, and, chagrined, she kept quiet during the slow withdrawal of the rest of the balls, shivering as each one left her body following a last teasing roll along those sensitive tissues. Randy released her hands with the last ball and helped her up. Falling against him, she relished his thick arms coming around her, his wide chest to rest against, and the steady, reassuring beat of his heart beneath her ear.

"Sorry. I just wanted to repay you for all you've done for me."

His deep baritone rumbled above her, washing through her battered, confused feelings. "All I've ever asked of you is your trust, Mickie, which I plan to test now."

Mickie didn't need the tug on her hand to follow him across the room. Her heart thudded with remorse. It was true all he'd ever asked of her was to trust him. She'd been a rebellious handful when they first met, and she'd done nothing to change that even after he'd promised to care for Black Jack and invited her to help. His parents had treated her unruly, independent behavior with kindness, and the hired hands would shake their heads with amused tolerance. She'd fought against Randy's authority, frustrated concern, and protective caring until she'd let herself believe those traits meant more than they did at the time.

She thought she'd learned the hard way how naïve she was about reading people's intentions toward her when she'd returned following college to find him committed to Melanie, hearing how he still thought of her as the kid he'd befriended and nothing more. But in just these past few weeks of living with him and opening herself up again, she discovered her deeper-than-friendship feelings had been there all along, and could believe he needed to go through the wrong relationship before he could see she was no longer the neglected, pitiful kid he'd taken under his wing.

They walked past Amie strapped face-up on a padded bench, her face flushed, tight nipples gripped in clamps, a double dildo embedded in both orifices as Ben trailed a multi strand flogger up the inside of her thigh. Ben winked an emerald eye at Mickie, snapping the leather strips with a flick of his wrist as Randy stopped at the star-shaped, wooden structure next to them. Her pulse tripped with a one-word command that took her mind off the other couple.

"Strip."

Remembering to trust him took less effort but still didn't come automatically, and she vowed to work on that as she unhooked the bra and handed it to him. It was then she noticed the black bag next to the contraption that was only slightly taller than her five-foot-six and the lube-shiny anal beads hanging from his belt loop. Why she found that more embarrassing than shimmying out of her skirt and thong and standing there buck naked, she couldn't figure out.

Lifting her chin with his knuckles, Randy said, "Turn off your busy mind."

"Easier said than done," she returned ruefully as he backed her against the smooth wood.

"Try. This is called a St. Andrew's Cross Spider and was added after I sold out. I haven't tried it yet, so this will be a first for both of us."

Standing right in front of her, he drew her arm straight out to the side and attached a cuff to her wrist at the pointed end, making it easy to see his nipples through the mesh section of his leather tee. She made a mental note to tease the small brown nubs first chance she got. Thinking about that pleasure distracted her from the slide of his rough, denim-covered cock against her bare mound then the tingles racing under her skin after he bound her other arm and stooped down to restrain her ankles. Left exposed with her arms stretched out to the side and legs spread in a wide vee, she kept her eyes on Randy when he dove into the black bag and pulled out a blindfold. Instead of uncertainty assailing her, relief chased away her tension. She could relax more and give him that complete trust he wanted if she wasn't distracted by others or with trying to read Randy's expression.

Randy eyed her bound body with appreciation, lifting the blindfold to tickle the sensitive skin along the underside of one arm. "I like the shape of this cross, and how you look on it." He dangled the blindfold in front of her eyes. "Any complaints or misgivings?"

"Nope." Mickie shook her head. "Not a one."

"That's what I like to hear," he returned with approval, placing the black silk over her eyes.

Mickie sighed, leaned her head back, and

embraced the darkness knowing neither he nor anyone else here would let anything happen to her that she didn't want. He didn't waste any time throwing her body into sensory overload, running his calloused palms from her shoulders down her chest, plumping her breasts then tweaking her nipples until the pressure drew a low moan. Heat took a zipline down to her pussy where she spasmed with empty neediness.

"Ra...Master Randy," she murmured on a tortured groan, finding those pesky rules hard to follow as he circled her belly button then delved between her legs with a multi-fingered thrust.

He put his lips to her ear, swirling his fingers inside her. "Mmmm? Want more, do you?"

Her hips jerked as he made a slow withdrawal that tormented her pulsing clit. "*Yes.*"

His deep chuckled reverberated in her ear and held a note of triumph. "Hold that thought, Mickie."

Small prickles raced across her damp skin when he moved away, but the sudden snap of something small and leather on her right nipple erased them with the fiery pain. "*Fudge!*" she cried out, not sure if she was brave enough to let him continue until he soothed the ache with a soft, feathery stroke. "*Oh,*" she sighed on a shuddering breath.

"See how easy it is to put yourself in my hands?"

Randy kissed her, his unshaven jaw scratching her cheeks, which meant the warm breath on her sore nipple and lips that closed over the throbbing tip weren't his. Her immediate reaction was to shy away from accepting someone else's touch, but Randy was quick to allay her misgivings.

"Let yourself go. We'll catch you," he whispered above her lips, sliding his hands behind her to knead her buttocks.

Not trusting her voice, she nodded and once again leaned her head back, trusting him like never before. The other man remained quiet, and Randy only spoke to offer praise or encouragement as they touched, kissed, and licked every inch of her body. They would pause to use the slapper then the feather, the sharp stings tempered by a soothing caress, each intended to drive her higher and higher to that plane where nothing mattered but the overwhelming pleasure building deep inside her.

Mickie whimpered as hot breath scorched her nipples followed by dual deep suctions, and she decided there were definite merits to the extra mouth and hands. She went rigid with a searing smack on her tender labia and melted in spiraling ecstasy as soft lips relieved the pain. Randy's whispers abraded her thighs as he spread her folds and lashed her clit with his tongue, his partner nibbling on her arched throat while thumbing her nipples.

Sensations bombarded her from all angles, prompted by light pain, calming strokes and kisses, lapping tongues and nibbling bites. They waited until she was beyond coherent thought, beyond the point of no return, beyond caring who did what as long they delivered before Randy's raspy voice reached her ears.

"Come for me, Mickie."

It was the emphasis he put on *me* that tossed her over. Bright lights and white stars exploded behind the blindfold, her climax lighting up the inky darkness, the intense pleasure tossing her adrift until she collapsed in Randy's strong arms.

Randy nodded his thanks to Neil who sauntered off with a two-fingered salute. He didn't want Mickie to be uncomfortable around Neil when they saw each other again, which was why he'd asked him not to say anything. He scooped up her clothes, leaving the blindfold on as he carried her upstairs, past the grins and thumbs-up of well-meaning, encouraging friends. The way she'd given him her complete trust after realizing he'd invited another man to touch her had driven him to a heightened state of urgency. He would reassure her later, when he could think straight, of his limitations when it came to sharing.

For the first time in the fifteen years he'd been involved with the alternative lifestyle, small pinpricks of jealousy were poking at him by the time Mickie climaxed from their dual torment. As much as he'd enjoyed bringing her to that point where nothing mattered except letting go, he would let her know it was a one-time experience.

Only one door remained opened upstairs, and Randy strode into the private room, dumping Mickie on the large, four-poster bed without bothering to close the door. She didn't wait for him to remove the blindfold, whipping it off to reveal gray eyes darkened with renewed lust. Her gaze shifted from his hands releasing his engorged cock to the open door, her face flushing redder as the club's activities echoed upstairs from below.

Using his teeth, he ripped the condom open, grinning when she looked back at him and sucked in a deep, chest-lifting breath. "Hurry," she demanded, bending and spreading her legs as she slid a hand down to cup her palm over her labia and lay her middle finger between her creamy slit.

"I didn't give you permission to touch my

property," he said, anticipating and enjoying her instant reaction to his inflammatory comment when her eyes flashed with ire, her mouth slashing into a tight line. "Careful," he warned, coming down on top of her. He shoved her hand aside and slide inside her wet heat. "I'm still in charge and don't want to have to reprimand you again tonight." Pulling out of her snug clasp, he tunneled back between her folds, working his way inside her again until he lay balls deep between her wide, soft thighs. "*Ahhh,*" he sighed, dipping his head to lick her jumping pulse. "Like coming home."

"I can't stay mad if you're going to say something like that." Mickie arched against his groin, drawing her legs around his lower back and her arms over his straining shoulders. "I prefer you naked, but this will do. Are you going to make me beg again?"

Her voice held a hint of whining, which made him smile against her neck. "No," he rasped as she clenched her vaginal muscles around his cock, "not this time."

As he reared up on his arms, her hands fell to grip his forearms, and he proceeded to ride her like a man possessed. Having gotten to know every nuance of her body these past weeks, he was prepared for her quick build-up of arousal as she spasmed around his thrusting shaft. His head roared with the pleasure of her fiery heat licking up and down his length, and he savored her soft cry of release as much as the tight squeezes that pumped his orgasm forward. As he lost himself in her again, he wished for once it would last longer then doubted his ability to maintain control if it did when he spewed into the latex with deep, shuddering breaths.

****

Randy was signing the last payroll check when he heard Mickie coming down the hall. She rarely slept in past seven-thirty, let alone nine o'clock, and he credited her exhaustion to the strenuous night before at Spurs. He looked up from his desk at her knock, taking in her well-rested face and small smile curling that tempting mouth.

"Good morning." He beckoned her forward with his fingers. "Any side effects from last night?" he asked, eyeing her tight body in snug jeans and tank top.

"No, should there be?" she asked, tilting her head, her hair pulled back in its customary braid.

"Not necessarily, but there often is. Your active lifestyle has kept you strong and in shape, which helps." Sliding her check across the desk, he hoped she was pleased with the amount. "It's payday, and..."

"What is this?" she snapped, picking it up and glancing at the check. "This is way more than your mother offered." Her whole body practically shook with the outrage in her tone.

Baffled, Randy leaned back in his chair, placed his elbows on the armrests, and steepled his hands under his chin. "I'm taking over the books, as you know, and gave you a raise. You've done a good job..."

Throwing the check at him, she interrupted his explanation again with a sneer. "Fucking you? Did you offer to pay all your women for their services? If so, no wonder you couldn't hold onto any of them."

Outrage she would think so little of him brought him to his feet, the urge to shake some sense into her too strong to trust himself getting any closer. Fisting his hands on his hips, he returned her piercing glare. "If you can believe that, maybe I should have listened when you insisted this change in our relationship would never work."

Her breathing hitched as hurt crossed her face. Mickie rarely let her emotions show, and he experienced a raw stab of guilt, berating himself for forgetting her insecurities even though he'd hoped they were well past these misconceptions.

"Maybe we both should have. Lance just called me. There's a bull down up north. We're driving out to check on him." She spun around and headed for the door.

"Stay with Lance," he reminded her in case she let her anger with him overrule caution.

"I'm not an idiot, at least not where my safety is concerned," she replied without pause or turning around.

Randy sank back down on the chair, muttering, "Oh, you're an idiot, kid, make no mistake." He would give her time to stew, and, with luck, realize her error before she returned. If not, he would set her straight on several things.

Chapter Thirteen

Mickie stomped out to her truck, fighting the tears blurring her vision. She'd given Randy *everything* last night, the trust he'd insisted on since they started this ill-fated affair, and what did he do? Offered to pay her! How could she not be both pissed and upset or view his raise as anything except a reward for sleeping with him? She hadn't held the foreman's position long enough to earn a bump in salary, having just started when he returned.

Working to get herself under control, she drove down to the stables and picked up Lance, ignoring his cheerful smile as she took off the minute he got in and shut the door.

He flicked her a curious look, grabbing the side handle as she sped across the uneven terrain. "Bad morning?" he asked.

"You could say that. Taking this job was a mistake." She hadn't meant to say that, but it was what she was thinking and just slipped out.

"Why? I thought you loved the ranch."

"I do." She always had, ever since Randy had brought her back with him and offered to let her help take care of Black Jack.

"C'mon, Mickie, give. I don't want you to quit, and neither do the guys."

Mickie slowed down, taking it easier as she drove the fastest route to the northeast pasture. She should be thinking about the downed steer, not her hurt feelings. "I don't want to leave, but I can't...he *paid* me," she finished under her breath without intending to say that aloud.

Lance's expression turned puzzled. "Well, yeah, he paid everyone this morning, and said he gave everyone a raise. Didn't you get one?"

She jerked as if struck, which she might as well have been. "Everyone got a *raise*?" she choked, gripping the steering wheel as remorse and chagrin went through her on a wave of guilt. How could she have been so stupid, jumped to the wrong conclusion without thought?

"That's what he said when he sent a text early this morning. He said the quarterly returns were better than projected, and how much he appreciated all our hard work. The Daniels are great to work for."

Mickie crested a rise and spotted the black Angus in the valley, lying between the pond and the woods. She never checked her phone this morning and didn't give Randy much of a chance to explain. She was trying to come up with a way to apologize to Randy and make amends when she pulled next to the large bull, wondering if her insecurities had just cost her everything that had ever mattered.

Lance reached over and pressed her hand. "Don't cry – the boss will kill me!"

"What?" She blinked rapidly, drying her shimmering eyes. "I don't cry, so don't worry." No, she only made a fool of herself and spoke without thinking because she was too afraid and insecure to accept an act of generosity without question or suspicion. She'd jumped the gun, ready to believe the worst of Randy in order to protect her heart, which, she admitted, was more vulnerable following her father's betrayal when he'd raised his hand against her for the first time.

That's no excuse, she thought, reaching for the door handle. She could only hope to find a way to make amends when she returned to the ranch if it wasn't too late. "Who called in the injury?" she asked Lance, looking at him as she opened the door.

"Some hikers on Eagle Trail using binoculars.

The ranger station contacted us after getting their call and seeing the location was on our land." Lance scanned the field and surrounding woods as she left her seat. "Stay close to the truck—" But Mickie was already out, stooping to examine the steer's hind leg when Lance's warning was cut off by the report of a gunshot and her startled cry of pain. "Mickie, get down!"

The burning slice across her upper arm was the only warning she needed to scuttle behind the still-open truck door, her heart pounding against her chest, her throat dry with fear. The bull let out a scared low and struggled to stand but couldn't and went down after hobbling two steps. From what she could see of his injury, it looked like a possible knife wound, which meant this was a setup. Her blood went hot with rage, cursing the Carbello brothers, whom she suspected were behind this sabotage, and herself for failing to give Randy the only thing he'd ever asked of her — her complete trust.

"Can you get a message out?" Mickie asked Lance, reaching for her rifle he slid across the seat.

"Already done. The radioed SOS went broad, so not only will the sheriff's office and rangers get it, but every ranch within the perimeter. All we have to do is hang tight until backup gets here."

Several more shots pinged against the truck, one shattering the windshield. "*Fudge* – is that all we have to do?" she returned, gasping and covering her head.

"Sorry, spoke too soon." Lance reared up and fired several shots toward the forested hills, in the direction of their antagonist. Hunkering back down to avoid the retaliated response, he panted, "We need to get to the cover of those trees." He nodded to the east, the dense woods several yards from the truck. "How fast can you run if I cover you?"

"As fast as I need to, then I'll take over for you." Seeing that as their only option, she gave him a reassuring smile. Her flesh wound had turned numb, which helped as she sucked in a deep breath, willing her nerves to hold up until Randy arrived, never doubting he would risk hell and high water getting out here. Where had her faith in him been earlier today? Shoving aside that regret for later, she nodded at Lance. "On the count of three."

Lance returned her nod. "One, two, three – go!"

****

Fear-pumping adrenaline propelled Randy out to his truck, his booted foot flooring the gas pedal as soon as he put it in gear. He never should have let

Mickie leave believing he would pay her for sex. He'd let his anger-based disbelief get the better of him, a first and last for him. She was smart, he kept telling himself, and both she and Lance were crack shots. If he didn't think they could hold off their attacker until help arrived, he wouldn't trust himself. That didn't mean he wasn't praying with every breath for their safety.

God help the person or persons threatening his girl and hired hand.

His radio crackled with responses from the ranch community, but he only listened with half an ear as he concentrated on getting to the stables, making sure the rest of the hands had arrived and were preparing to help before getting to Mickie. Seconds after he roared to a halt and breathed a sigh of relief seeing the hands already in vehicles, on ATVs or horseback, another car pulled up, and he swore as Ed Taylor got out with a determined look.

"Where is she?" he croaked.

"I don't have time for you now. Wait here until we get back," Randy snapped, signaling for the others to start out.

"Tough. She's my daughter, and I'm going."

He'd picked a hell of a time to remember that little fact, but Randy didn't have time to argue.

Another vehicle came barreling down the drive, and he recognized Steven's worried, grim face behind the wheel. Pointing to Ed as Steven got out, he said, "Ride with Steven, and stay the hell out of my way. Thanks," he tossed at his former foreman, knowing Steven would understand his urgency.

"Go," was all he said, all he needed to say.

Randy jumped behind the wheel again and tore out right behind the others. Bracing against the jarring drive across the open range, he took note of who was responding and where. From the location and direction of shots Lance was able to send, they knew it was likely either Dex, Chuck, or both perched on the ridge above the northeast pasture. Shawn and his deputies were enroute to head them off if they fled, setting up a barricade on the back road, Route 6, cutting off their only option for escape by vehicle. There were enough ranchers and rangers combing the woods if they were dumb enough to flee on foot. No one knew the forests and surrounding land better than those men and women.

Once he ensured Mickie's safety, Randy intended to set her straight on a few things. He refused to let her continue to hide behind her insecurities, regardless of her surprising acceptance of Melanie's visit, or whatever other excuses were flitting around her head to keep from committing herself fully to him and a future together.

The sporadic reverberations from gunfire reached him through the open window as he followed Ned and Toby past Mickie's abandoned truck and the downed bull to the edge of the woods. Whipping their vehicles perpendicular with the trees to give them more coverage, he breathed easier when Lance lifted a hand from behind a tree, his thumb pointing up.

A round of shots struck both their trucks as he and his hands ducked out their driver's side doors and returned fire, the loud racket from multiple guns exploding in the air. When the clamor died down, the sudden silence was almost deafening to Randy's ringing ears.

"Everyone okay?" he barked, not relaxing until he heard everyone's voice, especially Mickie's. "Don't move," he warned them, waiting to see if their assailants realized what a bind they were in and were smart enough to stand down.

Five full minutes passed before the radio's static interrupted the eerie quietness that had settled around them. Even the injured bull's frightened lowing had ceased.

"We've got one perp in our sights, and we're

on his ass," Shawn announced, sirens wailing in the background. "He's headed west but won't get far."

"Neil and I have spotted Chuck Carbello hightailing it in the same direction from the south," Ben said.

"I have enough deputy backup. Dakota, Clayton?" Shawn inquired.

Dakota's hard, clipped tone came through next. "We're headed your way, Ben."

"And when we get these bastards, it'll be my pleasure to nail their asses."

The last of Randy's tension slipped away hearing Clayton's determined vow. The DA possessed a well-deserved reputation for being a ruthless prosecutor who rarely settled for less than a maximum sentence. And when someone came after one of their own, he went for the jugular.

Keeping a tight grip on his rifle, he stood and headed toward the trees and Mickie, but paused, bracing himself when she came flying toward him and flung her arms around his neck in a stranglehold he was in no hurry to break.

"I...I'm sorry," she choked out, her breath hot on his neck, her body quivering against his. "I shouldn't have thought that, said that."

"No, you shouldn't have. Damn it, Mickie."

He tightened his arm around her waist. "You have to stop thinking you don't need anyone, that you're happy keeping your distance."

She lifted her head, and his heart turned over at her crooked smile. "Why?"

Instead of chuckling, like he knew she intended, he growled above her lips, "Hell, Mickie, because I love you, and want you to love me just as much, that's why."

The shakiness in Randy's whispered breath, his words, uttered in a stricken, gravelly tone reached a place somewhere deep inside Mickie she'd kept closed off from everyone, including him. Emotion, thick and heavy, welled from that protected place, the words no one had ever spoken to her before breaking through the locked door. His thick arm held her so close, so tight she struggled to take a breath, his heart thudding so hard against hers she couldn't decipher the beats between them. No one had ever been there for her before him. He'd stood up for her all these years against her parents, yesterday against his ex, and today against this threat.

The damp sheen burning her eyes since she saw him come to her rescue spilled over as a tortuous sob pushed past her constricted throat. Shocking them both, she broke down into a bout of uncontrollable weeping, her hands clinging to his shirt as she rambled without thinking.

"I...I didn't think I...stood a ch...ance against what you...had with Melanie. I'm not...like her...or any of the...others."

Randy gripped her braid and tugged her head up, but she couldn't read his expression through the waterfall pouring from her eyes. "Fuck, Mickie. She may have been my wife and submissive, but you?" He brought his hands to her heaving shoulders and gave her a small shake. "You're everything."

How could two such simple words hold so much meaning, carry such a wealth of unburdening importance to her very soul? "I'll never have your way with words," she said, working up the nerve to tell him how she felt.

He shook his head, and she soaked up his deep rumble as he replied with the exasperation she was used to hearing from him when he spoke to her. "All I need is to hear you love me."

Mickie let go of a lifetime of insecurities and crumpled against his familiar strength, for the first time in twenty years giving him the second thing he'd ever asked of her. "I love you, Randy."

A round of applause came from the guys as

Randy skimmed his hands down her arms in a slow caress. "It's about time – what the hell?" Mickie savored his angry concern when he noticed the flesh wound on her arm. He dropped the f-bomb again, pulling off the bandana Lance had wrapped around the bullet graze. "Why didn't you say something?"

Mickie realized he wasn't talking to her when Lance answered. "I didn't dare over the radio, and, in case you're unaware, you two have been locked together since your arrival chased off our sniper."

Laying a hand on his bristled cheek, she worked up a reassuring smile despite the annoying waterworks that wouldn't stop and teased, "It's only a scratch, and that's twice in a row you said –"

"Yeah, yeah, not a nice word. If you don't want to hear it, quit pushing me into cursing."

"Company," Ned announced as another truck came to a halt.

Mickie gave up counting how many shocks for today this one made when she gasped, "Dad?" Randy went rigid, pivoting to shield her, but she slipped around him to stand at his side, watching her father and Steven get out, both with looks of concern and caring. Seeing a sign of tears in her dad's eyes for the first time weakened her knees, forcing her to grab onto Randy's arm.

Ed cleared his throat. "You're okay?" he asked, his gaze sliding from her face to her arm.

"Yes, thanks to everyone." She still couldn't believe he was here, coming to her aid in a time of dire need.

"Good, good." He emphasized each word with a nod then looked at Randy, and no one could doubt his sincerity when he said, "Thank you."

Mickie knew he wouldn't forgive her dad as easily as she always had, but before she could say anything, Steven tipped his hat back and winked at her. "All grown up and still getting yourself into mischief, girl. Why don't we take this party back to the ranch? It's past lunchtime, and I'm hungry."

Mickie sniffed and brushed her hand over her tear-streaked face. "I could eat two of Randy's quarter-pound hamburgers, but let me see to our bull first. Poor guy's been through the wringer."

Randy grinned at everyone. "She doesn't let anything interfere with her appetite or her work."

Basking in the pride in his voice, Mickie embraced the new path forward they were taking together, confident she could hang on to the best thing that ever happened to her.

****

Two months later

Leaning her arms on the corral fence, Mickie went hot all over watching Randy lasso the darting calf then jump off Cheyenne with a boyish grin creasing his bristled face. Shirtless except for a leather vest, his sculpted chest glistened with perspiration as he hog-tied the calf and then pumped a fist in the air in triumph to the applause from everyone gathered around the enclosure.

She laughed, shaking her head as he lifted his Stetson and raked his fingers through his sweat-dampened hair before releasing the bawling young Angus. "He's still a kid at heart."

"All men remain boys at heart, and I wouldn't have it any other way." Caroline's eyes sparkled as Randy's mother slid her gaze toward his dad who congratulated Randy on breaking the day's record for the calf-roping contest with a hearty slap on the back. Looking at Mickie, she asked, "Are you feeling okay? You look peaked."

Despite the inner heat watching Randy always generated, Mickie experienced another wave of nausea, the same annoying ailment having plagued her for a few days. "I'm fine, just the touch of a summer bug. I'm not going to let it ruin the day. I've been looking forward to hosting this month's picnic, and everyone's put in a lot of work to make it a success."

All the neighboring ranches took turns putting on the summer picnics that drew not only their families but the residents of Mountain Bend. Given the high August temperature this afternoon, the Daniels had opened their doors, inviting everyone to set their covered dishes on the tables set up in the den buffet style. People were already filing in to fill plates to carry back outside and sit at the long tables in the tree-shaded yard. The trek down to the corrals didn't deter some from carrying their food that far so they could watch the livestock activities. Other traditional picnic games such as horseshoes, tug-of-war contests, and three-legged races were taking place on the lawns, laughter and squeals of excitement echoing through the air.

"It's been a huge success, and I do believe we have a record turnout." Caroline cocked her head at Mickie, a small grin tugging at her lips. "I have to reiterate how pleased Ron and I are with your engagement. It came about much sooner than I thought."

Mickie sent her a sharp glance, the smug expression on her future mother-in-law's face setting off a light bulb. Straightening from the rail, she pointed a finger at her. "You knew he was returning when you offered me the foreman's job."

"Guilty, but not until a few hours afterward. I gotta admit, my boy's timing was perfect."

"You couldn't have known we would get together." The way she'd fought against the change in their relationship, Mickie couldn't imagine Caroline noticing something between them before they'd left on their trip.

"Oh, sweetheart." Caroline laughed. "*Everyone* thought you two belonged together and would eventually work your way around to where you finally are." She eyed the sparkling diamond adorning Mickie's finger since last week. "He does have good taste, in both jewelry and women, at least now. I never could abide Melanie. She was too shallow and self-centered to make my son happy."

"He says I'm a pain in the ass." Given the butt blistering Randy had heaped upon her last night when he'd seen her name on the list of contestants for bronc riding today, she'd have to beg to differ. Because that led to a bout of exhilarating, outdoor sex was beside the point.

"Yes, but he says it with indulgence instead of exasperation. You ran him ragged those first few years," she reminded her.

Mickie shrugged. "He was away at college for most of that time."

"Face it, Mickie, the sparks were there for years once you got into college, but back to your nausea." Her gaze turned earnest. "Are you sure it's a bug ailing you?"

The sudden nausea had already disappeared, having come and gone as fast as the other few times. "Sure, what else...no, no way," she denied when she realized the direction of Caroline's thoughts. "We're careful..." She remembered the hot tub sex at Spurs last month when she'd begged him to take her hard and fast, so desperate for release she hadn't wanted to wait for him to suit up, thinking it was a safe time. "Oh, *fudge.*"

As Caroline threw her arms around her in delight, Skye and Amie strolled up with curious expressions. "Hey, we wanted to see your ring, but is there something else we get to congratulate you for?" Skye asked.

Mickie dislodged herself from Caroline's embrace, still too stunned about the possibility of being pregnant to think straight. She'd just wrapped her head around getting married. There was simply no time to deal with another life-changing event, and that was that. "No, no there's not." She thrust her hand out to show them her ring. "Just this. We're planning a Christmas wedding."

"That might be a little too long, dear," Caroline murmured.

"Why too long? Ben and I will have taken six months when we marry in October." Amie's face transformed from puzzled to a flush of excitement. "Oh – *really*?" she squealed, taking over where Caroline left off in hugging Mickie.

No, no, no, she kept denying even though she returned her friend's well wishes. "That's great, Mickie," Skye enthused. "I'll bet Randy is thrilled."

"Not a word from any of you." She glared at each of them. "I'm not sure, and Caroline has jumped the gun here. Promise me."

"I give you my word," Caroline said. "I won't tell Ron until you're sure and tell Randy."

Amie nodded. "We won't, either."

"At least the trial will be over by the end of the year. That will be one less thing to worry about. I hope you're not upset Clayton refuses to offer a plea bargain. Speaking of my husband..." Skye waved at Clayton as he sauntered into the corral, next in line for the roping event.

"Oh, wow, he's wearing chaps." Amie fanned herself with an exaggerated sigh.

"I'll leave you girls to ogle. I need to get back up to the house and help Betty."

Mickie waited until Caroline was out of earshot before saying, "No, I'm not worried about testifying, Skye, not with Clayton's guidance. Randy will be there also."

The Carbello brothers had been picked up within fifteen minutes of being spotted that day eight weeks ago, and they'd wasted no time lawyering up. After the trauma they'd put those three horses through, not to mention herself, and the bull they'd cut with a knife to draw her out there, she was happy to have a hand at putting them away for a long time. Of the three states prosecuting the men, Idaho was the only one adding two counts of attempted murder charges to their horse-theft crimes.

Mickie had always heard it said things happen in threes, and along with putting those two away and her upcoming marriage, the third positive spin on her life had come from her father. Forgiving him hadn't come easy, but witnessing his efforts to change had gone a long way in that direction. He'd humbled himself to get a desk job at the mill so he could complete the required thirty years to get a pension. She still didn't visit him alone, without Randy, but when they did go, the trailer was looking better, and he hadn't shown signs of excessive drinking. There was evidence he still imbibed too much for her liking, but at least he was trying and holding on to this second chance at the mill.

"Speaking of hot guys." Skye nodded over Mickie's shoulder.

She spun around to see Randy approaching with his usual swagger, the rope coiled and hanging from his side, a cocky grin flirting around those sensual lips and the straw he chewed on, her usual damp response clutching her pussy muscles. Apparently, the possibility of pregnancy didn't curb her lust, thank God. She lifted a hand in an absent gesture to Skye and Amie telling her they would see her later, her focus centered on the man who still annoyed her with his bossy overprotectiveness, but she wouldn't trade for anything. From the moment she'd flagged him down on the road and enlisted his help with saving Black Jack, she'd been his. It had just taken her twenty years and a threat to her life to come to terms with it, and to believe someone could care about her, love her the way he did.

As usual when he leveled that potent, dark-eyed look on her, everything and everyone around them fell to the background. Their neighbors' voices and laughter, the clomp of horse hooves, the lowing of cattle, and the tantalizing whiff of barbequed meat carried on the slight breeze were glossed over by Randy's tall frame blocking her vision, his earthy scent filling her nostrils, his gleaming, bulging muscles spiking her temperature, and his low voice drawing a shiver of awareness along her skin.

"I'm not sure I'd recognize you if you ever decided to try going clean shaven," she stated, loving the rugged, disreputable appearance his scruffy whiskers gave him.

Randy rubbed a hand under his chin and along his jaw, his gaze turning warm. "Can't. My fiancée likes the scratchy abrasions too much to risk her wrath."

"Is that so? How do you know that?" she teased, running a hand down his chest.

He stepped closer and grabbed her wrist, holding her hand pressed against his pectoral. Leaning down, he nipped her lower lip, whispering, "From the way she sighs, moans, gasps..."

"Okay, okay, I get it. Be quiet." She backed away with a laugh.

"Get a fucking room, you two," Dakota grumbled as he and Poppy walked by. He tempered his comment with a slap on Randy's back. "Congrats."

"Yeah, same here," Poppy called back as her husband tugged her along.

"Thanks." Randy grabbed Mickie's hand and started toward the house. "I've worked up an appetite. Let's go fill our plates." He paused to catch a Frisbee then spin it back to the young boy.

Seeing an opening, she cast him a sly glance as they resumed walking. "I learned a long time ago you were great with kids. At least that's one concern I don't have going forward."

"Why would you –" He halted abruptly, his face dumbfounded until a slow grin revealed his acute pleasure. "Just when I think you can't surprise me again. Are you sure?"

"No, but your mother is." She laughed at his wince.

Randy pulled his gaze off the woman who had become his entire world to the gathering of friends and neighbors on his land. He hadn't believed life could get any better than these past weeks with Mickie, but it seemed there was more in store for them yet.

He couldn't wait.

The End

ABOUT BJ WANE

I live in the Midwest with my husband and our Goldendoodle. I love dogs, enjoy spending time with my daughter, grandchildren, reading and working puzzles.

We have traveled extensively throughout the states, Canada and just once overseas, but I now much prefer being homebody.

I worked for a while writing articles for a local magazine but soon found my interest in writing for myself peaking.

My first book was strictly spanking erotica, but I slowly evolved to writing steamy romance with a touch of suspense. My favorite genre to read is suspense.

I love hearing from readers. Feel free to contact me at bjwane@cox.net with questions or comments.

MORE BOOKS BY BJ WANE

VIRGINIA BLUEBLOODS SERIES

Blindsided
Bind Me to You
Surrender to Me
Blackmailed
Bound by Two

MURDER ON MAGNOLIA ISLAND

Logan
Hunter
Ryder

MIAMI MASTERS SERIES

Bound and Saved
Master Me, Please
Mastering Her Fear
Bound to Submit
His to Master and Own
Theirs To Master

COWBOY DOMS SERIES

Submitting to the Rancher
Submitting to the Sheriff
Submitting to the Cowboy
Submitting to the Lawyer
Submitting to Two Doms
Submitting to the Cattleman
Submitting to the Doctor

COWBOY WOLF SERIES

Gavin
Cody
Drake

DOMS OF MOUNTAIN BEND

Protector
Avenger
Defender
Rescuer
Possessor

SINGLE TITLES
Claiming Mia
Masters of the Castle: Witness Protection Program
Dangerous Interference
Returning to Her Master
Her Master at Last

CONTACT BJ WANE

Website
bjwaneauthor.com

Twitter
twitter.com/bj_wane

Facebook
www.facebook.com/bj.wane
www.facebook.com/BJWaneAuthor

Bookbub
www.bookbub.com/profile/bj-wane

Instagram
www.instagram.com/bjwaneauthor

Goodreads
www.bit.ly/2S6Yg9F

Made in the USA
Monee, IL
29 March 2022

93746337R00174